PRAISE FOR M.

The first...of (a) stellar, long-running romantic suspense series.

> — BOOKLIST, THE 20 BEST ROMANTIC
> SUSPENSE NOVELS: MODERN MASTERPIECES.
> *THE NIGHT IS MINE*

Top 10 Romance of 2012, 2015, and 2016.

> — BOOKLIST: THE NIGHT IS MINE, HOT POINT,
> HEART STRIKE

One of our favorite authors.

> — RT BOOK REVIEWS

Buchman has catapulted his way to the top tier of my favorite authors.

> — FRESH FICTION

A favorite author of mine. I'll read anything that carries his name, no questions asked. Meet your new favorite author!

> — THE SASSY BOOKSTER, FLASH OF FIRE

M.L. Buchman is guaranteed to get me lost in a good story.

I love Buchman's writing. His vivid descriptions bring everything to life in an unforgettable way.

AT THE QUIETEST WORD

SHADOW FORCE: PSI ROMANCE

M. L. BUCHMAN

Buchman Bookworks

Other works by M. L. Buchman: *(* - also in audio)*

ABOUT THIS BOOK

Delta Force operator Ricardo Manella *nearly died in the Honduran jungle. But while captive in a drug lord's camp, he discovers a unique talent that saves his life.*

Michelle Bowman *never thought about saving lives until a previously unknown telepathic connection to Ricardo saves his.*

However, her old college roommate's twin brother proves he possesses other powers—especially the skill to consistently piss her off.

When they become involved in a security test gone bad, they must depend upon each other and their unique method of communication to save both of their lives.

CHAPTER 1

*R*icardo lay in the mud where the horse had tossed him and tried to ignore the cold rain slashing down on him. He still held his rifle securely in his hand, not that he had any live ammo for it. If he had to lie here much longer, he might use it as a club on someone—soon.

Just another day in Delta Force, he kept telling himself.

Except he wasn't in The Unit anymore.

This was all Isobel's fault. Not the leaving The Unit part, but all the mud and rain part.

Why don't y'all come up to Montana? And, like naive chumps, they all had. When the great film star Isobel Manella called, everyone came—even her twin brother. Which somehow meant that he'd ended up crawling facedown through the near freezing prairie mud.

One of the stuntmen on her movie had driven the thirty miles from the shooting location, here in the wilds by the steep mountains of the Montana Front Range, to the nearest bar in some hole called Choteau. He'd gotten into a predictable brawl with the locals last night, and was sleeping it off with one arm in a cast and the other handcuffed to a hospital bed. Some Hollywood Joe-boy taking on a bar full of Montana ranchers. Not the brightest dude.

Her director had needed five-ten of lean Latino dude about the same moment the Shadow Force's plane had landed…and he'd been volunteered.

The fake rain—that the water truck had clearly tapped directly from a glacial stream, maybe straight from a glacier itself—made the quagmire far colder than should be possible on a hot June day. If it didn't stop pounding him deeper into the frigid mud soon, he was definitely going to have to hurt someone. Not Isobel, of course. Not only was she the movie's star, but he'd long ago learned (probably while still in the womb) to never try to outsmart his twin.

Her skills as an empath had cut off every nefarious plan a twelve-minute-younger twin brother could come up with before it even hatched—they'd split midnight between them and she'd been lording the extra "day" over him ever since to explain her "natural superiority."

:You look so cute.: Michelle's voice bubbled into his brain. And there was his first target.

:Go to hell!: Telepathy had its uses; telling off Michelle Bowman was a good one.

:You wish. You do look seriously cute though, Manella. Great butt. Which is about all that's showing above the mud.: She sent an emotion tag of *:(So laughing.):*—because no emotional tone passed over their link, just the words and timing. Over the last year, with her thoughts constantly rattling in whenever they chose, he'd learned to punctuate most of her sentences. She always chose the tease over the straight line, sarcasm over…most anything.

He pushed himself up just enough that he could see her standing close behind the director. Even mixed into the crowd of male and female ranch hands gathered to watch the movie being made on their property, Michelle still stood out.

Five-ten of sleek auburn redhead in jeans, a flannel shirt, and blue cowgirl boots—because, of course, she was always dressed perfectly for any occasion. She offered him one of her electric smiles.

He let himself drop back down into the mud. *Do not be thinking about that woman.*

Michelle scowled at him, but since that was one of her natural states, he couldn't begin to figure out why.

Besides, telling himself off didn't help. And the cold mud wasn't enough of a distraction. To a former Unit operator, this really was nothing. He'd take this any day over an Indonesian mangrove swamp crawling with eight kinds of nasties before you even started counting the critters that weren't carrying guns.

He began belly-crawling forward per the script.

Someone grabbed his hand, and it took all of his strength to not reflexively take them down hard. He was supposed to be the battle-battered hero wounded in a Wild West ambush after all.

Isobel, wearing the wet look like perfection, helped him to his feet. She slung his muddy arm over her shoulders. At least they hadn't dressed her in one of those white blouses that went transparent when wet. Izzy certainly had the figure for it and he appreciated that they hadn't taken the cheap shot. It saved him having to beat the shit out of the director.

"Remember to keep your head down. You look nothing like Javier," she whispered as he limped out of the mud straight toward the camera.

"Right. I'm much more handsome." But still, he wasn't the newest hot-guy movie star and Javier was.

His own shirt, however, was paper-thin, torn in all the right places, and bloody—with more red leaking from the small bladder under his arm and trickling down his chest.

"I've got better pecs, too."

Ricardo could feel Izzy's half laugh where her arm was clutched around his waist, though of course she didn't show it.

He used the butt of his lever-action Winchester 1873 rifle like a four-foot-long crutch as instructed. It was a crime to do such a thing to such a great old gun, but this was Hollywood recreating the Old West and he assumed they were too stupid to care.

They dragged forward until he was afraid they were going to walk square into the lens before the director yelled, "Cut."

In moments, they were both swarmed by aides for this, that, and the other thing. All he needed was a dry towel and a fresh shirt, but instead he was pushed into a shower stall on a truck that appeared to be there just to provide shower stalls.

Fresh clothes and towels were waiting for him by the time he was clean.

As he stepped back out, some damn fool tried tackling his hair with a blow dryer on a long extension cord. He waved the kid off, half hoping he'd go electrocute himself in one of the many wet spots left over from the scene shoot. But it wasn't going to happen, because there was some other chick tending the cord to make sure it stayed dry and no one tripped on it. Behind her there was—

Isobel was looking dry and perfect as she met him outside the trailer and led him over toward an actual chuck wagon, complete with wooden wagon wheels and a red-and-white checked canopy. Someone was already pulling a jacket on over her shoulders. It wasn't hers—some rawhide thing that maybe was appropriate for a gunslinging woman in the Wild West—so probably for her next scene. She shrugged to settle it into place with an elegant gesture.

The food was anything but authentic, and it smelled

seriously good. The chuck wagon must be part of the ranch location rather than the movie. He hadn't had a chance to look the place over yet, some fancy-ass dude-ranch horse spread.

He did grab a spare towel while they waited in line and began wiping down the rifle that he'd also rinsed in the shower. It was habit. A Unit operator's life often depended on the condition of his weapon, so it always got second priority, after any dangerously bleeding wounds. Minor injuries, food, sleep…all those came third.

"You really need all these people?"

"Do you pay for more support staff or do you shoot for more days? On big films, bodies are cheaper than time." Isobel went for the healthy stuff, of course. Just to make her whimper, he loaded his plate with sausage buried in peppers and onions, a big side of potato salad and chips, then threw a couple of fried chicken breasts aboard for good measure (a favorite of both of theirs).

"More bodies are especially cheaper if they've got your big sister the star on the payroll," Michelle appeared by Isobel and fingered the rawhide. "I want your jacket."

"Wrong shape for you, Michelle." The two of them traced all the way back to being college roommates. The jacket had definitely been custom-made to show off his twin's curvy figure rather than Michelle's sleek one.

"I want it anyway."

Ricardo imagined what Michelle would look like in a similar rawhide jacket…and nothing else. She also had really good arms. Maybe sleeveless. *Should buy her a vest like that, dude.* And…maybe he should go soak his head back in the ice-cold mud puddle.

Instead he took a bite of chicken, then set his plate down while waiting for a shot at the brownies. He chewed and focused on drying off the Winchester. If he could scare up a cleaning kit, he'd do it properly rather than trusting some hack of a prop guy.

"I always like a soldier who takes care of his weapon," someone handed him a BoreSnake kit as if reading his mind.

Ricardo almost dropped the long Winchester, then snapped to attention out of habit. "Colonel Gibson?" He nearly spit his lunch on his former commander.

The man who never smiled, still didn't. "Master Sergeant Manella."

"What the hell are you doing here, sir?" He swallowed hard and nearly choked himself. He didn't know why he bothered asking. Colonel Gibson was the commander of Delta Force and was probably the best soldier who'd served in The Unit's spectacular forty-year history. He also had a habit of silently appearing at the most unlikely of times.

"My wife and I are retiring here," he nodded in the direction of the main ranch that lay up against the break of the Montana Front Range.

"You're married?" He'd never imagined the colonel married; he was such a pure hard-ass soldier that it was hard to imagine him as anything else.

At that the man almost did smile. "And I thought my retirement would be the big news."

"No sir." Ricardo shook off his surprise. "That's simply unimaginable. I find that to be way past the friendly lines of mere surprise. So you being married is the only thing that fits within my personal range of what I would classify as surprising."

Michelle—who'd been purposely blocking the brownies just to piss him off—looked at them in wonder. "I don't know who you are, Colonel. But you just made him string together more words than he's used since birth."

"Like you'd know," Ricardo really didn't need her sassing his former commander.

"She wouldn't, but I would." Isobel held out a hand and Gibson shook it firmly. "She's right as usual, Ricardo, and you know it. A pleasure to see you again, Colonel."

"Again?" Ricardo hadn't even known that his former commander knew *about* his twin, never mind actually knew her.

"Let's have lunch and talk," Colonel Gibson nodded to where the other three members of their team were already eating.

:This is gonna be fun,: Michelle teased him.

:Careful or I'll make you swim in the mud.:

:You first. Oh, wait. You already wallowed like a pig facedown in slop. Besides, if you try, I'll sic your big sister on you and then you'll be sorry.:

Which almost made it tempting to try.

He wished he could mentally shut her out, but he hadn't found a way yet.

Ever since he'd busted through whatever barrier had spared him from her internal voice for most of his life, she could project her words inside his head and he couldn't do a thing about it. His only vengeance was that he could do the same—if only he could ever think of what to say to her. There were times he wished he could scream at her to stop, but it would sound just as atonal as everything else they said to each other this way. He couldn't even sleep through it if she spoke "at" him in the middle of the night.

A flunky came up to take the rifle from him, but scampered away when Ricardo snarled at him. He pocketed the cleaning kit, tucked the rifle in the crook of his arm, and picked up his plate. Together they threaded their way through the crowded fold-up tables and chairs over to the one wooden picnic table where the rest of Shadow Force: Psi had gathered.

There were six members of Shadow Force, the only six in the world—that they knew of—with psi powers.

Isobel was both movie star and empath.

Michelle's stepbrother Anton, an Army helo pilot who towered as big as a Montana grizzly, could "see" remote places.

Just a couple weeks ago they'd picked up another pilot— Jesse was a Texas cowboy and a Night Stalker helo pilot who stood almost as tall as Anton—and his now-fiancée Delta operator, the little slip of a blonde Hannah Tucker. Together they did strange things with sound projection.

Talk about a motley crew: movie star, four ex-soldiers including himself, and whatever the hell Michelle was.

Just as he sat, he realized that Michelle's ploy had worked —he'd forgotten to grab a damn brownie. He knew exactly what she was.

Total pain in the ass. Ricardo nodded to himself. *Yep! Dead on.*

MICHELLE TOTALLY HEARD his silent voice message. Just to tease him, she kept her smile on her face and didn't respond as Ricardo sat down across the picnic table from her.

But he didn't react or even glance at her as he usually did when they were speaking into each other's heads with their telepathy. Instead he focused on his meal.

And it had felt different.

Not tone exactly but…different.

An internal thought? One not meant for her?

Did that explain the "Should buy her a vest like that, dude"? Was she herself the "her" in that thought? It was difficult to imagine Ricardo giving her anything other than the hard edge of his tongue on the few occasions when he did speak.

Did this mean that he could hear her own internal thoughts if she didn't consciously direct them at him?

That's a majorly cute ass, Manella. Which was true of all of him actually. He was fantastically fit.

No response.

So, she could hear him, sometimes, but he couldn't hear her unless she directly thought at him.

That meant that inside his head he'd called her a "Total pain in the ass. Yep. Dead on."

"You're a real asshole, Manella."

Everyone around the table turned to look at her. She shouldn't have said it aloud, even if it was true.

He simply looked at her with those beautiful dark eyes of his that also told her nothing of what he was feeling, even when she could hear him thinking.

His shrug came with no explanatory internal dialogue. It was as if he agreed with her.

"Glad to see your team is shaping up well," Gibson picked up a hamburger with all the trimmings as if they were all one big happy family. He'd said it so deadpan that there was no way to tell if it was sarcasm or not.

Isobel, who would know through her empathy, simply smiled as she cut a slice off a grilled chicken breast. "Yes, I'm pleased."

"Your team's rescue of Ambassador Delaney has received praise at the very highest levels."

"Which would be yours, except you said you're quitting. What's up with that, Colonel?" Ricardo glanced down the table at Hannah Tucker.

:What's up with the look?: Michelle sent to him.

:I've been out of Delta most of a year. Hannah just left a couple days ago; thought she might know.:

:You were still in while in hospital and rehab.:
:Thanks for the reminder I didn't need.:

He'd finished the last of it just a few months ago—a full year after his rescue. Only after the docs had declared him healed to the best of their ability had he been medically retired. Isobel had told her how hard it had been for Ricardo to leave The Unit, not that he'd ever admit it.

:Either way, I've been out. Hannah left Delta less than forty-eight hours ago to join Shadow Force: Psi, so maybe she would know…:

Michelle spotted Hannah's infinitesimal shake of her head.

:What's the problem, Ricardo?:

His shrug was no bigger than Hannah's head shake. *:Man's an institution.:*

:And he's retiring. People do that, you know.:

Still, Ricardo looked freaked, so she turned to take the bull by the horns.

"What are you going to do after you retire, sir?"

Colonel Gibson's smile was slow, but it made her think that his wife was a lucky woman if she got to see that smile. "I was hoping you'd ask."

Michelle wondered if that was a good thing, but then she overheard Ricardo's internal dialogue: *Oh shit!*

She didn't need to see Ricardo's sun-dark skin paling to know the emotion behind that thought.

CHAPTER 2

"*I* have only a little time while they set up the next scene," Isobel commented as she ate some chili.

Michelle had been enjoying her own until Ricardo's comment. A moment ago she'd wondered if she'd ever really tasted chili before; it looked so simple and tasted so complex. Now it tasted like old sandpaper.

She'd enjoyed going on the little missions the team had done before.

When it had been the four of them—her with Anton, Isobel, and Ricardo—it had almost felt like family. Bickering, squabbling, teasing family, but family.

With Hannah and Jesse on board, they'd taken on their most serious mission yet, rescuing the US ambassador. It had been exciting…until the Congo's presidential guards had started trying to kill them with machine guns.

Michelle hadn't peed her pants, but perhaps only because of Mom's constant tirades on always have clean underwear in case you were hit by a bus and had to go to the hospital. Ironically, her mother had been the one to be hit by a New York metro bus. Thankfully not very hard, but enough to be sent to the hospital for cracked ribs and a fractured arm. Michelle hadn't asked, but she'd wager Mom's underwear had been perfect.

Now here was Colonel Gibson, Hannah's and Ricardo's former commander, sitting with them. That meant that Shadow Force's assignments weren't going to get less dangerous any time soon.

Though Isobel was right, her lunch break was almost over.

Already various workers were hurrying away from the tables and back to set the lights and cameras for whatever the next scene was. A long boom on a flatbed truck, a trio of small camera drones, and a helicopter with a herd of racing horses painted along the side said it was probably a riding scene. She'd often gone riding along as Isobel had practiced daily for months in preparation for this film. Now she looked as if she'd ridden her whole life.

Michelle had enjoyed starting out with her, but Isobel had dusted her soon enough—she was five-ten, Isobel was only five-six, but Isobel was the one who could swing up into the saddle from standing on the ground as easily as if climbing a set of stairs.

:It's your fault,: she shot to Ricardo.

:What this time?:

:You're the one who taught Isobel to be such an athlete.:

:Nah. She was the natural. I had to learn to keep up with her. Never take her on in soccer.:

:I'm wicked at soccer.:

Again one of those strange pauses in Ricardo's speech as he looked at her before continuing.

There were times she wished she could read his mind, not just hear the thoughts he chose to send—and a few of the ones he apparently didn't.

Ricardo was still thinking hard, but she didn't hear a

thing. Was he picturing something? Their telepathy didn't include images any more than it did tone. Was he picturing her in a soccer outfit? If so, she was gonna smack the man but good.

:You've been warned,: he finally sent.

"We need to have a soccer match tonight," she challenged the table just as Gibson was starting to say something. His glance at Ricardo said that he hadn't missed that there was some byplay going on.

"You're not a telepath, are you?" Michelle asked Gibson in a whispered aside.

"No. I have none of the gifts that your team exhibits."

"But…"

"But I am a practiced observer of human nature." Then he cracked that smile again. "The ranch doesn't really have a good space for soccer, but they do enjoy volleyball."

"Fine; volleyball then," Michelle declared aloud.

:She's even better at volleyball.: Ricardo might smile even less than Gibson, but she could see the amusement in his eyes. And now he'd be picturing something else?

:Isobel is five-six! She can't be better at volleyball.:

:Setter, not spiker. That's if anyone can stop her serve.:

"Definitely volleyball," she declared anyway.

"I like a woman who isn't afraid," Gibson said softly. "There is something about fierce bravery that supersedes all other skills. It is far easier to teach the latter rather than the former."

"He must like you, to speak so many sentences," a tall, elegant blonde stepped up to the table but didn't sit. Michelle could only think of her as majestic: fit, steady, and somehow just what every woman should be though she wore clothes no fancier than Michelle's own—far less so actually. "Colonel Gibson is rarely so loquacious."

"This is the team I was telling you about. Everyone, this is Major Emily Beale."

Michelle wasn't a big fan of how Ricardo was looking at her. Then Jesse's fork hit his plate with a clatter as did Hannah's a moment later. They were definitely the cutest couple she'd ever seen.

Jesse then whispered something to Anton, who softly said, "Holy fuck."

"What?"

No one responded.

Michelle looked up at Emily. "Who are you that you scare the crap out of my semi-brother?"

"Semi-brother?"

"I'm trying that label on instead of half-half siblings. Our parents married; then divorced, married others, and had us separately; and finally divorced again to remarry each other. Anton and I were both about three when they got back together. It made us some kind of siblings—even if I'm a stunning redheaded and he's just a towering hunk of black dude. And before you ask, step-siblings is just too lame and doesn't begin to cover our relationship's weirdnesses."

Emily's nod said that she accepted the explanation probably as calmly as she did everything.

"So back to my earlier question," because something about this woman made Michelle curious to know more about her. "What about you scares my six-foot-five semi-brother into silence?"

"I don't think that 'scare' is quite the word you desire. That would be the *colonel's* role in most endeavors," she rested a hand lightly on Colonel Gibson's shoulder. "I am merely one of your hosts, as this is my husband's family ranch." Her casual wave encompassed everything from the big ranch house with its horse barns, cabins, corrals, and all, over to the jagged mountains that punched aloft to mark the start of the mighty Rockies that seemed to be carved from the achingly blue sky.

Anton whispered across the table to her. "Remember I told you about the flying legends, the two majors of the Night Stalkers that I always used to dream about flying with?"

Michelle shrugged a yes. It hadn't really stuck out in her memory, but Anton had always been talking about "The Majors" like they were gods who deigned to walk the earth.

"That's her!" He pointed a finger like he was afraid the woman might bite him. And wasn't standing right there listening with an amused half-smile.

Not once in all the years had she seen him cowed in the presence of another. Not even Isobel, with her unstoppable beauty and smooth Latina accent had affected Anton.

Yet he was utterly overwhelmed to be in the presence of Major Emily Beale.

"You keep abashing my semi-brother and I could get to like you," Michelle announced.

"Deal." Emily held out a hand and Michelle shook it firmly.

"Of course, we'll see how you feel after we've talked. Why don't you all come down to the house tonight after the filming is done for the day? I'll let our chef know you'll be joining us."

"Tell him he's worth swimming in mud for," Ricardo held up a brownie that she was sure she'd blocked him from getting. Then she looked down and saw that one of the two she'd taken to tease him with was gone from her plate.

Michelle snorted out a laugh.

And for some reason, that's what finally made Ricardo smile.

～

IF HE COULD EARN one of Michelle's laughs just by wallowing in mud and stealing a brownie, it might be worth repeating. If he could get her to wallow with him…That was seriously entertaining thought. One that sustained him through an afternoon of watching Izzy gallop back and forth across the Montana prairie, cameras rolling.

She trotted happily with the too-handsome leading man, Javier. Ricardo didn't watch the kissing-on-horseback scene —or its infinite retakes—because there were some things that a man should never have to imagine, like someone manhandling his big sister.

Michelle, unstoppably, gave him a running commentary on it as soon as she noticed his discomfort.

Later, Isobel galloped away from the bad guys in a long leather duster.

She rode at a full gallop, with no reins, and rose to stand in the stirrups and fire a rifle with the techniques that he'd taught her about the proper handling of firearms.

So damn proud of her I could bust.

:Then tell her, you big oaf.:

:Leave me alone, Bowman.:

He hadn't realized that he was thinking "aloud." He'd have to watch out for that. Having Michelle able to talk directly to him alone was already strange enough.

Finally, as evening fell, Isobel raced through the water truck's "rain" shower—off to save the townspeople from something or other. This time they took the cheap shot of the thin, wet blouse, but the failing light would hide the details. Some of them. At least a few.

Shit! Teenage boys are gonna go wild for that scene.

:Every man with a heartbeat will, and a whole lot of women. Your sister rocks!:

Shit! Had to be some way to keep Bowman out of his brain.

16

And through the whole day, he also did his best to not watch Michelle, but images of her on horseback. Of her in his arms. Of her lying—

A year ago he didn't even know who she was. "Michelle" had just been the name of Isobel's decade-gone college roommate and nothing more.

Ricardo had gone straight into the Army out of high school. He'd done it partly to honor their father and partly to help Isobel's future. Papa had gone down in the Gulf War and Mama was a single-parent nurse. There was only enough money to send one of them to college and he knew from early on that Isobel was the one who'd be important if given the chance.

Turned out he'd been right. Texas A&M Performance Studies had been where she'd belonged. She'd been scouted for films right out of a college production for a sexy girlfriend role. Then they'd discovered that inside her stunning body was a total tomboy and Hollywood had finally found that perfect combo of incredibly sexy, total kick-ass action heroine, *and* "ethnically diverse"—a phrase designed to piss them both off.

But, whatever they called her discovery, within three years she'd proven herself as a major talent and now they were writing movies specifically for her. Her career hadn't slowed down since.

By the time she offered to pay for any schooling he wanted, he'd been applying for Delta Force. *That* was the school he'd wanted. And for a decade it had paid off in full… until that day in Honduras when it all went wrong.

The drug-runner's runway had been a narrow strip of dirt in the middle of a slash-and-burn operation. They were running Cessnas, Beavers, Pipers…all crap single-propeller planes. The strip was too short for even the Beech King Airs and twin Cessnas, never mind the small jets. It was a rinky-dink operation, but someone had to scout it and take it down.

He hadn't screwed up. It was scant comfort, but what went down hadn't been his or his teammate's fault.

Ricardo and Del had perched high in a tree and tracked everything going on along the runway and throughout the adjoining camp until a family of howler monkeys decided to set up nearby and start screaming at each other. Some *chico* barely old enough to wield an AK-47 had dumped an entire magazine blindly into the treetops to kill the monkeys. They'd just swung off, uninjured, howling and gibbering the whole way.

With three rounds in him, Ricardo had plummeted down to land almost at the *chico's* feet. What came next was too ugly to remember and during that time he'd often envied Del's single clean round through his chest. Didn't take a genius to figure out they were American Spec Ops, so rather than just killing him, they'd dragged him off into the deep jungle, staked him out, and gone in for some torture.

It had been coming on dusk.

Then…

:You okay?:

The question inside his head had sounded clear as a bell. He'd been wishing he could see Izzy just once more and the words had just snapped in—but in no voice he'd ever heard before.

:Ricardo?:

No, that wasn't what had come next. It had been—

A hand rested on his arm. Then it shook him.

He swung his forearm at it—hard—to knock it aside. As he made contact, he turned his hand to capture the thin wrist and leveraged his assailant to the ground with a sharp twist and a pressure point. He raised his other hand to strike down and break their neck when there was a shout in his head.

:Hey! That hurts!:

On her knees in front of him, a bounty of lush auburn hair streamed over the attacker's face. Just like the sadistic Consuela, who'd taken a special delight in breaking a rib or another fingerbone each time she could get at him in that Honduran hellhole.

Except Consuela's long hair had been black and curling.

Not red.

She was—

He'd—

:Oh Christ!: He let go of Michelle's wrist. *:Oh God, I'm so sorry. Are you okay?:*

:I'm fin—:

It was all he had time to hear before Anton's massive fist connected with his jaw and sent him flying backward into a large cloth light-diffuser panel. It collapsed as he tumbled backward through it, plowed into a lighting instrument, and knocked over several people.

Someone screamed.

Another yelled, "Cut!"

The tangled group of film people collapsed and clattered to a standstill with him at the center. He'd just started to extricate himself from the mess when Anton plucked him up by his shirt like a rag doll and dangled him high in the air.

"Give me one reason not to break your punk ass."

As if he had one. He'd just attacked…

He couldn't even think it.

Been ready to kill…

He let his head drop, *Oh God, I'm so sorry for so many things.*

"Put him down, Anton."

Ricardo squeezed his eyes shut. That was the worst. Michelle not taking the slice out of him that he so richly deserved.

"I'm gonna bust him up so bad that—"

"He's already been there," her voice was soft but intense.

"Shit!" Anton dropped him back onto his feet. Anton knew better than anyone what condition Ricardo had been in by the time they'd extracted him from that jungle—he'd been the pilot of the helo and had taken a round himself as part of the rescue.

Ricardo had needed more operations than he had fingers and toes—even if you still counted the three toes that had been cut off. More bits of titanium in him than bones. Left hip and shoulder and right elbow weren't even his.

Sure, he'd been Delta Force…at least some of him had.

Now he was nothing.

:Ricardo?: It was easy, too easy to imagine the gentleness of Michelle's question.

:Don't! I couldn't! That was unforgivable.:

He turned and walked away as fast as he could. His body had healed enough to let him escape. But his mind never would.

No way could he tolerate her understanding or, worse yet, her pity.

"IF YOU DON'T GO after him, I'm going to kick your ass so hard that you'll end up in Canada." Isobel hissed from close beside her.

"It's not that far. Canada is pretty close from here." But Michelle didn't turn. She could only watch as Ricardo disappeared into he movie crowd.

"You want me to try?"

Michelle didn't. But she didn't know how to go after Ricardo either. It was one of the drawbacks of telepathy. She *knew* that he didn't want to be followed.

Suddenly Michelle's butt hurt. Isobel's kick had landed plenty hard to send her stumbling forward—almost falling into the half-resurrected lighting equipment.

"Hey!"

"Listen up. First, I am going to reshoot that scene you two messed up. I was so close to done! Then I'm going to shower. *You* are going to find Ricardo. We'll meet you at the big house for dinner. Until then, don't mess with me."

When Michelle didn't start moving, Isobel raised her foot threateningly again. Michelle went…about two steps.

"No way!" Now Anton blocked her way. "Not after what he just did."

"It will be okay, Anton. Just let me go."

"Nope!"

"Want me to sic Isobel on you?"

"Won't matter," he declared and crossed his big arms over his chest, but he was watching Isobel out of the corner of his eye.

"Do you want to mess with *me?*" She pushed up onto the toe of her periwinkle-blue boots and rested a hand on the center of his chest.

He still didn't give way.

"How about both of us?" Isobel asked. Except the sweet Latina was gone and her voice had a tone that sounded as if she just might enjoy taking down a man twice her size.

"Now, ladies. I—"

"We're not any kind of ladies, Anton. Now let her go."

With a final grimace, he moved about a quarter-step aside.

The director came up. "We're ready to reshoot that last sequence. If no one else interrupts us." He scowled all around him.

Michelle took advantage of the moment and dodged around Anton.

Except Ricardo was nowhere to be seen.

By asking, she managed to track him around sound trucks, equipment trucks, star trailers, bathroom trucks, a massive generator truck surrounded by a vineyard of fat rubber power cables, before finally breaking into the open near the horse barns. Away from the film lights and out into the Montana dusk, it took her eyes a while to adapt. The ranch had only a few lights, and those were mostly on the porches of the main house and cabins.

A longhorn cow stood in the middle of the dirt driveway, apparently napping in the fading light.

Michelle didn't know if it was by chance or not, but Emily, the blonde host from earlier, stepped out of the barn just as Michelle reached it. The woman didn't say a word, just nodded toward the open side door and kept walking.

The cow barely reacted when Emily paused on her way to pat it on the flat spot between its eyes. Apparently giant cows wandering around the yard like stray cats was a normal event on the ranch.

Inside the barn was a relief from the craziness of the film production. Here it wasn't only Isobel who smelled of horses. Everything did. To either side of the long central aisle were horse stalls. The aisle itself was packed dirt with a scattering of hay. It smelled of surprisingly clean horsiness. Even the high-end stables that she and Isobel had ridden from in San Antonio during Isobel's training for the film hadn't smelled this fresh. The mustiness of hot Texas days had gathered there; not here.

It wasn't hard to trace Ricardo. She couldn't feel him, their telepathy was limited to just words, but there was only one figure in the dimly lit barn with fewer than four legs. He slumped on a hay bale at the far end of the aisle.

His funk was so deep that he didn't notice her until she was quite close. When he did, he jolted to his feet, spun away, and walked squarely into the closed door at this end of the barn. Bouncing off, he landed hard on his ass.

Again he scrabbled to his feet.

:Do not (hard snarl) run away from me.:

He froze with his back to her.

She reached out toward his back.

:Don't touch me.:

She flinched—no need to hear his shout behind the words as she could see it in his abrupt hunch.

But she completed the gesture.

At the moment of contact, he slumped.

She could feel the heat of him against her hand. Beneath her fingers and his light shirt, the powerful ripples of his shoulder muscles shifted as he practically twitched beneath their simple contact. She knew that he'd been whipped, nearly to death several times, but feeling the long lines of scar tissue crossing her palm made her realize that it was the first time she'd *ever* touched him.

:Please don't.: It was barely a whisper inside her head.

:You're a mess, Manella.:

:Tell me something I don't know.: He slowly squared his shoulders until he stood up straight once more. She let her hand slip off when he took the single step away before he turned to face her.

"I'm sorry, Michelle. I would never intentionally hurt you."

"Duh!"

He managed a twisted grin for a moment, but wouldn't quite look at her, instead studying her left ear. Ricardo only used her name rarely. And then only her last name. Her first name told her just how badly he felt—out loud no less.

"I'm guessing I interrupted a bad memory."

:You were never stupid.: Even when she spoke aloud, he was far more likely to answer her silently.

She thought a lot about Ricardo—it was hard not to, with his thoughts impinging directly on her brain—but she'd tried not to think of those first days as she'd become the conduit of his rescue.

:*Who are you?*:
:*What's happening to you?*:
:*Where are you?*:
:*Who do I contact to come find you?*:

The spiral of unknowns and panic had escalated through six sleepless and utterly maddening days.

It had taken her time to batter through him begging her—if she was real—to get a message to his sister Izzy. Each time he regained consciousness, he returned to that like his sister was the only hope that still existed in his life.

After his rescue, Michelle became incredibly sad: not just for Ricardo, but for herself. Anton cared for her like any decent semi-brother would—or real brother, for that matter. But if his world came apart, she doubted she would do more than drift through Anton's thoughts. If that.

Ricardo worshipped his sibling.

Finally unraveling that his sister Izzy was Isobel Manella, who had been Michelle's college roommate for years before she'd become famous, had had her really kicking out the jams. She'd contacted Isobel to find Ricardo's commander *and* called Anton. Pure chance had Anton's unit doing a rotation on one of the Navy's littoral combat ships, which was just offshore Guatemala.

Her weird telepathic connection to Ricardo had let her guide Anton's ability to "see" remotely until his team could pinpoint the jungle base camp and take them down hard. Anton could always target "hidden" enemies with a pinpoint accuracy that had kept his crews and commanders in awe. He'd rained down hellfire on the drug lord's camp.

Ricardo had never really explained what had happened to

him aside from being a captive of a bloody-minded bastard. It hadn't taken a genius to know he'd been tortured.

For nine months he'd specifically asked her to *not* come meet him. She would have gone anyway if Isobel hadn't warned her off.

"For you to see him now… Shame is very hard for a man like my brother. You saved his life and he thinks you are some kind of angel."

They had both laughed, but it'd had an edge to it that had more to do with not crying than anything else.

Each time she reached out, wondering if the connection would still be there, he'd replied that he was fine. *Physical therapy. And I thought PT sucked when it meant physical training. This is way worse. (Laughing.)* They'd learned that, especially early on, they had to define the emotion; telepathy was worse than e-mail for communicating feelings. Now that they'd been inside each other's head for a year, em-tags—not even little emoji pictograms passed between them down whatever this strange channel was—weren't as necessary.

One time she'd contacted him just as he was coming out of recovery from an operation. The drugs made him more susceptible to actually telling her what was going on.

:Rebuilding my leg. Third time. Doc's saying…hang on…thinks he finally saved it. New shoulder next time.: She'd called in sick to work and kept him company as he faded in and out while lying in the recovery room but learned little more about what had happened. At least she knew he was alive. Perhaps it was just as well; there were some things she didn't want to know.

She did learn a lot about his sister though—more than she'd learned being Isobel's college roommate. Ricardo really did worship his twin.

Nine long months Michelle had waited to meet him.

In that time, she'd quit her job in retail—it was hard to

care about women's dresses after listening to the few tidbits Ricardo or Anton let slip about what had happened in the Honduran jungle.

Instead she'd become an EMT. She'd always been a good student when she cared, and this time, she had. Three weeks for EMT-Basic. She hadn't even noticed Intermediate going by on her way to EMT-Paramedic. For the nine months that Ricardo had kept himself sequestered, she'd worked on nothing else. It fueled her. She had some purpose at last. Double-shift ride-alongs to get her practical hours. Studying anatomy, symptoms, negative drug interactions, and more until she was ready to drop.

She hadn't told Ricardo, though she wasn't sure why. Maybe it was the same thing he was doing; she didn't want to have him discover "his angel" had been no more than a clerk in a high-end dress shop. She'd let him think that she'd always been a paramedic.

The problem was, they had this unique method of communication that required no more than a focused thinking *at* one another, but they'd both fallen into the habit of barely using it.

Now he stood with his back to the barn door as if awaiting a firing squad.

:*Goddamn it, Manella. Will you just relax?*:

He didn't shift at all until a horse in the nearest stall stuck his head out to sniff at Ricardo's shoulder. Finding no carrots or sugar cubes, the horse snorted loudly and Ricardo jumped.

How far in his head did a Unit operator, even a former one, have to be to not notice a horse-sized horse? The big gray retreated and silence slid back over the long barn.

Finally his eyes drifted to hers. :*I'm so sorry that—*:

:*Heard that already. Try something new.*:

He dropped down onto the hay bale. "I was back in the

jungle. The moment you touched me, I thought…"

"You thought someone had come to torture you some more."

Again, he inspected her carefully.

:Of course I know that's what happened. As someone just suggested, I'm not an idiot. Oh, wait, that was you.:

He dug his hands through his hair. He'd let it grow long until it spilled down to his collar. Michelle idly wondered what it would feel like slipping through her fingers. It added to the dark and dangerous look he wielded like Captain America's shield to keep everyone at a distance.

Without even noticing, she'd let it distance her as well.

IT WAS the one thing Ricardo had never wanted Michelle Bowman to know about him.

His weakness.

Pathetic man that he was, he'd shattered there in the jungle. Would have told them anything. Tried to tell them everything.

But they hadn't cared. All they wanted was his pain.

His body finally worked again, mostly. He'd tackled physical therapy with the same focus a Unit operator brought to every challenge. His minimum day now was three hours of workout and a 5K run. The pain was…manageable. The mental shit? He'd thought he'd had that blocked.

:I can't…trust myself.:

:That's okay, I trust you.:

:Just proved that shit wrong.:

:No.: Michelle leaned back against the horse stall. When the horse stuck its head back out, she reached out to scrub at the animal's cheek. The horse sighed happily and leaned into it. *:You proved it right.:*

27

:Bullshit.:

:Horseshit would be more appropriate to the setting.: Michelle petted the horse's nose, then sat down next to Ricardo on the hay bale.

He tried to scoot farther away, but he was already at the end and couldn't quite bring himself to running away again.

:I can prove it.:

:How?:

:With the way you're trained, how hard would it be for you to break my arm or even kill me?:

He could only stare at her in disbelief.

"Yeah, that's what I figured. But you didn't."

:Nearly did.:

"It's like being pregnant. You either are or aren't. You either did or didn't, and…wait for it, suspense moment…you didn't."

Ricardo propped his elbows on his knees and studied his interlaced fingers. He'd cut off his hand before he'd hurt her. The only reason the torturers hadn't already done that was they knew they could cause more pain if his hand remained attached.

His hands ached, as they hadn't in a long time. He'd done enough PT that they were as near normal as they'd ever be. But this time the ache was different.

All he could feel was how thin and fine Michelle's wrist had been in his grasp. How just the slightest bit more pressure would snap it. With the right twist, shattered bones would have sliced veins before punching through skin; she'd be bleeding out right now.

His hands had almost done that.

He'd almost done that.

Should have left me to rot in the jungle. That was one thing he knew for truth.

Michelle's hand touching his shoulder was like warm ice.

It soothed everything in its path and it chilled him to the soul. She was everything he wasn't.

He'd never been able to quite erase the angel image from his mind. In his delirium, he'd seriously considered the possibility that's what she was. Knowing she was a mortal woman, whom Isobel had occasionally mentioned in letters, was all that had separated her from supernatural manifestation.

He was a man destroyed in so many ways.

"Ricardo."

How was he supposed to ever live up to her standard? She'd saved his life.

All he'd done was leave everything he'd ever been in the jungle.

:Ricardo!:

:What?:

Michelle blew out an exasperated breath. *:It's time for...:*

Ricardo waited, half fearing she'd tell him to go to hell. He'd already been there. As Michelle's hesitation stretched out, he was unable to move, to think, to even turn and see what he might be able to read from her face.

"It's time for dinner," she said quickly, rising to her feet and taking a few steps along the horse stalls.

Like he could eat at the moment.

:She said for you to be there or she'd kick my ass. Again.:

:Again?:

Michelle rubbed her hand on her backside as if Isobel really had kicked her.

He couldn't imagine anything that would make Isobel kick her best friend.

:Now, Manella. (Stern command.) Let's go. Get your shit together.:

Not likely. But he didn't send that thought. He knew that was never going to happen.

CHAPTER 3

"You're telling me this is just a coincidence?" Michelle studied Emily Beale and Michael Gibson, who sat at the head of the table. "That Isobel just happens to be filming on your ranch *and* is on our Shadow Force?"

"Yes," Emily said it simply with no hint of another agenda as she passed the bowl of baked potatoes around the big kitchen table.

The room was a mash-up of a massive commercial kitchen, a table that could seat more than a dozen ranch hands at a meal, and a cozy seating area of couches and chairs around a big river-stone fireplace—unlit at the moment, but clearly well used. Everyone else from the ranch was apparently out at a big bonfire with the film crew.

The chef had left them huge platters of mushroom-stuffed pork chops, tomato-spinach quiche, and crusty bread still warm from the oven before going off to oversee the campfire cooking.

At the big table there were just Emily, Michael, and the six members of Shadow Force: Psi.

Michelle thought their new name was pretty cool, but a glance at the sullen Ricardo and she wondered how much longer the team would hold together.

Emily took her time chewing a slice of pork chop before she continued. "Our ranch has been looking for various ways to expand our income opportunities. Weddings, helicopter tours, cooking retreats with our master chef," she waved a hand at the spread before them and no one looked surprised. "Films were a logical next step considering the beauty of this ranch. A location scout tipped us that Isobel Manella was to star in the first big-budget Old West romance in years and we bid on the contract. I knew nothing of Ms. Manella's or your team's other skills."

"Then who—" Michelle cut herself off as Ricardo and Isobel, who were sitting across from her, both glanced at Michael Gibson.

He acknowledged their attention with the slightest tip of his head, but didn't speak.

Maybe Ricardo had taken lessons in "not speaking" from his former commander. Actually, now that she thought about it, Michelle rarely heard a peep from Hannah, the team's newest member, either. She too had been a Delta Force operator. Three Deltas. Including Emily, there were three Army helicopter pilots. Then Isobel…and her.

:Talk about being totally outclassed.:

:You (query)? Not. A. Chance.: Ricardo's thoughts sounded very emphatic.

:Look around this table.:

He actually did look around at Hannah and her cowboy fiancé, her own semi-brother Anton, even his own amazing sister Isobel, before focusing back on her. *:Not even a little, Michelle.:*

Again, her first name. It was impossible to doubt him when he did that, even if he was completely wro—

:I'm not just being nice—was never good at that. You shine.: Then he looked down abruptly, as if suddenly fascinated by his plate.

Michelle waited, but there were no other words, not even the spillover thoughts he believed were reserved for himself. If anyone else around the table had noticed their exchange, they were showing no signs of it.

She waited for her own reaction, but it was so slow in coming. Ricardo treated her like some crazy mix of angel, his twin's best friend, teammate, and toxic plague. He avoided her at every chance, but was it because of some crazy pedestal he had her up on? That fit way better than the other emotions she'd tried to fit on him: disdain, dislike, anger?

"Another aspect of Henderson's Ranch," Emily was telling the others, "is that we provide a certain type of security consulting to our government. The full knowledge of *that* operation is limited to three people. My assistant Lauren and I oversee that. Colonel Gibson wishes to create an action arm under that umbrella."

"Us," Ricardo said softly. "And why would you want us? *We* don't even know what we are yet."

"No one does," Gibson spoke for the first time. "You're the unknown in so many ways. I had never heard of anyone having such capabilities until Ms. Manella called to inform me of your call for help. Before I could respond, Anton Bowman was airborne with a strike force that should have been insufficient to penetrate the jungle. It was only as I was researching his record that I realized he, too, must have some uncanny ability."

"Seeing," Anton grumbled out.

"Seeing?" Gibson still didn't understand what her semi-brother could do.

"I can see shit that's hidden. Like I'm walking a path with

my eyes, but none of the rest of me is there. Can't hear or feel, but I can usually see just fine once I get a little guidance."

"Remote viewing," Emily said, as if such things were absolutely normal.

Gibson actually blinked in surprise. "What else don't I know about you five?"

"Six," Michelle didn't like being left out. Even if she wasn't special in any way like the other five, she counted too.

Gibson just scowled at her.

"I will *not* be dismissed out of hand. I'm—"

"Michelle," Isobel cut her off, "has never appreciated her own skills, or the fact that others can appreciate them. Your confusion is very apparent, Colonel Gibson; as apparent as Ms. Emily Beale's carefully masked perplexity—as if she's heard of remote viewing before. And no, Michelle, my brother Ricardo's absolute trust of you is not misplaced in my opinion either."

Michelle felt as if she'd just been kicked again. But not by Isobel's foot this time. No, the kick was somewhere in her head. *:You trust me absolutely (query / astonishment)?:* Then she added, *:(Total disbelief).:*

Ricardo's answering dark gaze required no words and left her helpless to respond.

"Don't you sometimes wish you could hear what they're saying to each other, Colonel?" Isobel continued complacently. "I can sense Michelle's deep skepticism and my brother's equally absolute certitude and yet I don't know *what* they are saying to each other. I only perceive the feelings they are saying it with."

"We," Ricardo finally looked away from her to face Gibson, but it didn't seem to release Michelle from her paralysis, "are not what makes this a team, Colonel. My sister Isobel is the essential sixth member. You need to integrate her empathy into your considerations. Also, that she is by far the smartest person at this table. No offense."

Isobel rolled her eyes, but Ricardo missed that as he was facing the other way. Then she leaned over and kissed her brother on the shoulder. Ricardo might flinch at Michelle's touch, but not at his twin sister's. No matter what he said, or rather didn't say, Michelle was something "other" so she triggered all of his body's alarms. Maybe it would be better to be overlooked.

"Six then," Gibson adapted quickly.

Michelle wished that she was a telepath with Isobel so that she could ask if he really had recovered so quickly, or if he was just good at masking it. Life would be so much easier if it *was* Isobel she was connected to. She understood Isobel, whereas Ricardo had enigma down to a fine art.

"This team…"

"Shadow Force: Psi," if she was a part of this, Michelle was goddamn going to fight for its identity. "Hannah and Jesse named us. That's who we are."

"Hannah did." "Jesse did." The two of them spoke simultaneously, continuing their uncontested quest for cutest Special Operations couple of the year award.

"The *six* members of Shadow Force: Psi," Gibson acknowledged with a slight tip of his head to Isobel, "include two of the best recon trackers I've ever met."

Ricardo looked up in surprise and Hannah twitched. Apparently praise was another thing that this Colonel Gibson didn't do lightly.

"I think that there are some real possibilities for the application of your talents."

"Which is why you pulled us together?" It seemed to be up to Michelle to keep carrying the conversation.

"Well, you had already self-identified. All I did was send Jesse and Hannah your way. I was no more sure of what they were than they themselves were. But I was hoping that the other four of you might offer them some guidance. As your successful mission to free the ambassador demonstrates, there is definite potential here."

"Civilians, Michael. This team includes two civilians," Emily warned him.

"If I had realized that you would take Ms. Bowman into the field, I never would have sent you into the Congo. I had been informed that Isobel Manella was expected here at the ranch, so I knew she was in the clear. By the time I realized Ms. Bowman hadn't accompanied her here, you were already airborne on your final leg into Kinshasa."

"And if you had tried to leave me behind, they and your precious ambassador would probably all be dead. We pulled that off by being a team." The words felt arrogant and she wished her temper would let her take them back but—

Anton muttered, "Damn straight, Missy." He was the only one with Missy privileges. Even though he said it too softly for Gibson to hear, she appreciated the encouragement.

:That's twice I'd be dead without you.:

Michelle wasn't exactly comfortable with that. But she and Ricardo had never found a way to lie in telepathy—other than just keeping their thoughts to themselves. It was like the words shorted out and hurt inside her head if they weren't honest. Even sarcasm was tricky—especially without any tonal markers.

RICARDO REALLY NEEDED to keep away from Michelle. The more time he spent with her, the greater the distance between them grew.

He'd managed to lose himself in the crowd still clustered around the campfire.

Gourmet s'mores and Montana craft beer reigned—the director had mandated no more than two of the latter, so these were carefully nursed. Ricardo snagged an Ivan the Terrible Imperial Stout. He preferred the nuttiness of a brown ale, but drinking from a bottle labeled Moose Drool was more than he could face. Who knew, maybe in Montana it really was brewed with moose drool.

He found a spot off to the side near a massive guy and his Malinois dog. Something about him said military, other than his broad shoulders. Male and military was good. Ricardo could deal with that even if he no longer belonged.

It was only one specific paramedic woman who was confusing the hell out of him and he'd be best off avoiding her.

"Ricardo," he greeted the guy.

"Stan," the other responded and reached out to shake with his left hand—his beer was in his right.

Ricardo twitched in surprise; the hand was cold. Not just beer-bottle cold, but definitely wrong—bloodless cold. He tried to apologize for the reaction.

"Forgot, sorry. Part of the deal. Gave up my hooks for a prostho arm. Don't worry, creeps me out still too." Stan's smile was grim and crooked on his scarred face. Then he waved it around in what appeared to be normal motion, even tried snapping his fingers—which didn't work well enough to awaken the big dog curled at his feet.

"Haven't got that down yet. It's an experimental rig I got snookered into. First time in years I can feel pressure and temperature. Nice to feel that a beer's cold," he switched the bottle into his left hand.

"That's…amazing. Too bad they can't fix the scars inside." Before he could be sorry about saying that, Stan was nodding.

"Yeah, those are a bitch."

37

They sat for a while beneath the stars. They shone clearly in the perfect sky despite the bright fire.

In a companionable silence they nursed their beers and watched the antics of the crowd. The cast, extras, and film crew all appeared to be doing some strange modern version of primitive mating rituals. A couple of people pulled out guitars and someone set up a couple of logs and some branches to drum on them. Soon the trio was doing a surprisingly lively version of Toby Keith's arrogant *How Do You Like Me Now?* A pair of sopranos and an alto picked up the chorus, then plunged into the second verse. Dancers began to boogie in the firelight.

Stan wasn't reacting much one way or the other. After watching for a while, he leaned down to scratch the head of the dog at his feet. "Dog did the first part of the healing for me."

"Saying I need a dog?"

Stan's shrug was unbalanced, as if…he was wearing a harness to keep his prosthetic in place. "Heard worse ideas."

Ricardo expected that his life was about to get busier based on the dinner's conversation. He didn't exactly see himself going all dog handler. Isobel and Mama had made sure that he grew up with cats in the house. He liked their independence.

Stan tipped his bottle to indicate a woman standing a quarter-way around the outer circle of people; there was just the slightest mechanical whir from his wrist as he did so. Another Malinois dog sat by her side as she spoke with a tall, gangly ranch hand wearing a cowboy hat—he looked too authentic to be an actor.

"What?"

"That's my best idea."

Ricardo kept an eye on her as he and Stan sat mostly saying nothing. At one point she turned briefly to aim a dazzling smile their way. "Assuming that wasn't meant for me."

"Not even a little," Stan was grinning back—a really surprising expression on his hard face.

All Ricardo could feel was shame.

"You'll get over it," Stan was now watching him. When Ricardo didn't respond, Stan continued, "It'll come back in bits and pieces when you aren't watching. Sometimes little pieces. Sometimes bigger," he scratched the dog's belly with a foot. "Sometimes a whopper," he didn't need to indicate the woman.

"In the meantime?"

Stan stared at the fire so long that Ricardo wondered if he was avoiding the question. When the woman turned toward them, her dog at an effortless heel despite no leash, Stan pushed to his feet. In a single heartbeat, his dog was up beside him and scanned in all directions for threats before relaxing.

"In the meantime," Stan paused to toss another log on the fire. "Try not to push too many folks away. Man needs his friends most when he thinks he doesn't."

When he walked away, all Ricardo was left with was the fire's heat and the cold stars.

CHAPTER 4

There were two more days before they were due to finish the Montana location shoot.

Gibson had apparently been content for the moment with their meeting over dinner and had disappeared again to who knew where.

No one came rushing to find Ricardo for some meeting. Javier was also a better horseman than he was, so, being done with dives into freezing mud puddles and a fierce brawl played out among a small herd of the neighbor's longhorn cattle, there was no further need for him as a stunt double.

Ricardo did his best to avoid…well…everyone.

So he worked out.

He ran with Hannah before breakfast. She was as quiet as he was—two Unit operators doing their thing who just happened to be near each other.

After the meal, while everyone else was drifting back to the set, he went hunting for some weights. He couldn't find a weight room, but he did find some old combine tires out behind the garage. Flipping a four-hundred-pound tire was a common enough workout for a Delta. He did that until his arms and legs burned.

Then some cowboy—with an accent that was half fake-Texas and half authentic-Long Island, New York—told him how to find the swimming hole up behind the guest cabins.

The man-made lake was empty. There were no regular ranch guests because of the film crew being on location. And they were all off filming a sex scene along some remote trout stream—something he really, really didn't want to see his big sister doing.

He even sent a few prayers for an out-of-season snowstorm or an unprecedented flood, but neither put in an appearance. *Figures.*

The entire ranch seemed to echo with the silence as big as the achingly blue sky. The "swimming hole" was a good fifty meters across. He was able to plow back and forth for ninety minutes until he'd worked up to 5K.

He lay on the floating dock in the center of the lake, shaking in the warm sunlight. It was a good shake: muscles pushed to their limits, shedding their lactic acid buildups in cathartic shudders. His body was finally back despite all of the pins and plates that had replaced so much of its structure.

"Me and Steve Austin, *The Six Million Dollar Man.*"

"I never found him particularly attractive. Too fake-Hollywood handsome."

Ricardo couldn't stop the shout of surprise. He also should have moved farther onto the float. His twist of surprise overbalanced him into the lake. He surfaced, choking out a lungful of water as he clung to the edge of the float. When he could refocus, he saw Michelle's laughing smile teasing him from the far side.

She had her bare arms crossed on the smooth wood and her chin resting on her wrists. The spaghetti straps at her shoulders hinted at just how little her bathing suit would be covering and he wasn't ready for that. He remained in the water on his side of the float, fervently hoping that she'd do the same.

No such luck.

With an effortless motion, she lifted herself up onto the float, stretching out on her side with her head propped up on one elbow to look over at him. At first blink, he was relieved that she was wearing a one-piece rather than a bikini. When he looked again, not so much. Michelle's long form was only emphasized by the red- and blue-striped material that stretched in very enticing ways over her curves.

"Am I really that scary?"

"Yes!" Not exactly his smoothest answer.

"Why?"

Not a chance he would try to answer that, despite the truth. *Because, if the Madonna was a redhead, she would look just like you.* A dead-inside man like him could never deserve someone like her.

"I'm not some saint. You know that, right?"

He wished that she didn't seem to read his mind so often. The telepathy was hard enough without that. Even stretched out there on the dock, he had no idea what was on her mind. *Messing with your brain, dude. That's what she's doing.* And it was seriously working.

Her sigh as she flopped onto her back didn't help matters at all. Stretched out on the dock, there was no way to avoid looking at her amazing form, revealed in profile by form-hugging Lycra.

:You doing this on purpose, Bowman (query)?:

:Partly.:

Well at least she wasn't playing coy. *:Fun to torture a guy?:* He regretted the words the instant they slipped out.

She tipped her head to look at him and he couldn't look away from those eyes as blue as the Montana sky. With her dark red hair turned almost black by the water, her eyes seemed even brighter and more piercing than normal. *:No. That's not what I'm doing.:*

:Right. Sorry. I shouldn't have said that.:

:I'm still hoping you'll be able to let go of all that some day.:

:Oh sure, just as soon as I stop having waking nightmares and then trying to kill my sister's best friend.: He could still see the bright red "bracelet" of where he'd grabbed and twisted her arm yesterday.

:Maybe if you stopped keeping it all locked up inside, then—:

:It already scares the shit out of me. Last thing I want to do is scare the shit out of you and everyone else.:

:What about—:

:Already had my dose of Army shrinks. So done.:

She closed her eyes and turned her face back up to the sky…but the sun caught in the glistening tracks of her tears. Oh crap. He'd made her cry; could he make it any worse?

He let go of the float, slipped silently underwater, and swam for shore in the dead silence of the pond's depths.

Why? Because he was a dogshit coward.

:CHICKEN!: Michelle thought when she opened her eyes and found herself alone.

If he heard it, and he must have, he didn't offer a response.

Damn you, Manella. But she kept that part to herself. The pain of seeing how wounded he was injured her nearly past bearing.

Michelle wasn't ready for who awaited her in the small gazebo that seemed to hover over the water by the shore. But there was no question in her mind that Emily Beale was waiting for her, even though she sat with her back to the water.

Swimming ashore, Michelle wrapped a generous Henderson's Ranch terrycloth towel around her hips, followed the water's edge over to the log gazebo, and sat down across from her.

Still Emily didn't say a word and Michelle felt strangely unwilling to speak first. Jesse and her semi-brother had been even more in awe of Beale than Ricardo and Hannah were of Gibson.

While she waited, she slowly became aware of sounds. The distant helicopter that must be part of the today's filming. Swallows that skimmed low over the lake catching bugs added the occasional flutter of wings, but mostly flew silently across the blue sky, adding sight rather than sound to the setting.

The sun moved the shadows of the gazebo posts before either of them added to either the motion or the sound.

"I like sitting here in the mornings when I can. I married Mark on this very spot a lifetime ago. I find it very reassuring."

Michelle wondered what Emily Beale needed reassurance about, but couldn't begin to guess. She kept the thought to herself and the silence stretched again.

"I often find civilians a little perplexing."

"Oh, like you military types make so much sense to us."

Emily smiled at that. "Both American, educated, motivated, yet such a divide lies between us."

"You mean between Ricardo and me."

"Between you and the rest of the team."

"You're forgetting Isobel."

"Isobel has other challenges to face," Emily said as if she was a clairvoyant who could read the future.

"I can hold my own."

"Take lessons."

"What kind of lessons? Could I learn anything that would have stopped Ricardo taking me down yesterday?" Michelle massaged her wrist unintentionally. The thoughtless power of him had been the most startling part of the whole experience. From Anton, she expected strength because he was so big. But Ricardo was her own height, and while not whip-lean, he wasn't broad-shouldered either. Yet his takedown had been as effortless as it was autonomic.

Emily's shrug was as enigmatic as her smile.

"From whom? You?"

"I wouldn't presume. Yourself perhaps? Life? Though you might learn not to shake a former Special Operations warrior while he's suffering through a PTSD attack."

Michelle felt the acronym slam into her gut. Of course it had been included in her paramedic training. Somehow she'd taken in the knowledge without the concept. Ricardo had been shattered in so many ways. Yet he'd rebuilt the external so thoroughly that she'd overlooked all the signs of the internal fractures.

Emily rose and stepped to the entrance to the gazebo. There she paused, but didn't turn back as she spoke. "Not many could stand back up after what happened to him. He's rediscovered the warrior—an incredible feat. But I wonder if he dares the next step, turning himself back into a man."

By the time Michelle caught her breath, Emily was long gone.

Who the hell did the woman think Michelle was that there was any way she could help Ricardo do that?

What *was* this place?

Michelle suddenly wished for a Russian invasion or something to get them out of here.

Ricardo intrigued and saddened her. That was all. Seriously! That. Was. All.

Yet somehow Emily Beale had implied that the next step in his future was somehow up to her.

No way, bitch. *I'm not a therapist, I'm a paramedic. He gets another hole in him, I can patch it, but that's where I stop!*

CHAPTER 5

"*H*ey buddy, you keep doing shit like this, you're gonna break yourself."

"Go fuck yourself, Anton." It was disheartening to see how effortlessly the big guy could grab and flip a combine tire. Helicopter pilots didn't need the kind of muscle a Unit operator did—or even a *former* Delta operator. Anton's innate strength was not to be denied.

Anton flashed a big grin that seemed as bright as the dawn's sun. Ricardo had decided that his best defense against his thoughts of Michelle was to keep himself damn busy on the last day of filming at the ranch. So he'd recruited the other two guys from the team.

After their run, they scared up a stack of old combine and tractor tires behind one of the barns. They'd been working up a good sweat working them along the line of the rail fence. None of them had noticed the two trainers working with a pair of horses in a nearby corral until he and Anton had peeled their shirts off and stuffed them in their back pockets.

"Woo-hoo! Now that's what I'm talking about!" A tall brunette called out.

"Shush, Lauren," a slender blonde—like the younger version of Emily—blushed brightly. But she didn't look away either.

"Maybe horse ranches aren't such bad places," Anton whispered far too loudly and grinned back at the two women.

"Sparklers," Jesse noted.

Sure enough, Ricardo spotted the sunlight glinting off their left ring fingers.

"Tough luck, Anton."

"Doesn't hurt none to look. Don't mind being looked at myself."

A tall redhead—with hair far brighter than Michelle's seductive auburn—trotted out of the barn to join the other two. Also wearing a sparkler, Ricardo noticed.

"Well, howdy!" She made a show of stopping her horse facing them over the corral fence. "Oh, how I do love the movies," she called over to her friends.

The blonde simply just turned and left through the open gate at a fast trot. The brunette followed close behind, but the redhead took the leisure of one more teasingly long look before winking broadly and turning to chase after her friends. All three sat their horses very, very well.

How would Michelle look up on a horse? Very easy to imagine—*Utterly exceptional!*

They turned back to their tires with renewed enthusiasm.

"They've got three like that here, then maybe there's more. Maybe even one to look at a poor shrimp like you, Ricardo."

All the friendly harassing that Anton slung his way helped distract him from his thoughts, but Ricardo didn't take as much joy as he'd expected from Jesse's struggles to keep up with them. Jesse might be powerfully built, but he had no idea how to flip a six-hundred-pound tire.

"Here," Ricardo went back to Jesse. "Low squat, straight back, arms outside your knees. Think of it like a barbell clean and jerk. Ready? Okay, explosive burst upward on three. When there's space at the most unweighted moment, step forward and get a knee under there so that the tire rests on your thigh. Shift your grip deeper for the jerk and push over the top, but be ready to scoot your ass backward in case it comes back on you. One, two, *three!*"

Jesse went for it and got it over with only a little help from Ricardo. By the third flip, he had the basic technique down. By the tenth he had it clean and was showing that he *did* have the right kind of strength.

"Make a warrior out of you yet, Jesse."

"Well, I can see how you might be thinking that," the cowboy blew out a hard breath and a grunt as he did the next flip, "but I'd rather be riding a horse any day."

"Why aren't you? This is a horse ranch after all. Must be a couple spare mounts around despite all that stuff my sister's doing."

"I'll be meetin' Hannah in half an hour for just that. Can't believe all the things she can do but still not know somethin' as easy as how to ride a horse."

"Not a lot of horses in Unit operations." Ricardo went back to flipping his tire to avoid admitting he found the big animals a little unnerving. Because Jesse no longer needed his guidance and Anton had already reached the end of the yard and was heading back along the fence line, Ricardo focused on what he was good for—flipping a goddamn worn-out tire.

"Need to be talking to your colonel about getting you

boys some proper horse training," Jesse gasped out another flip. He was still making too much work out of it, but there was only so far being a teammate went. A man had to do something to keep the upper edge over his buddies. "Think he'd bring back the cavalry? I'd wager that was something to see."

"Have you *seen* Gibson lately?" Ricardo hadn't exactly been trying to run into him, but better him than Michelle.

"Sure."

The loud *thump* of another of Jesse's flips came from behind Ricardo as he froze. He'd been told when he asked around that Gibson was nowhere around—back in DC maybe. But he hadn't asked Jesse until now. Gibson could apparently turn invisible in plain sight on a whim. How did the guy do that?

"Can't seem to turn around without tripping on him some. I'm thinkin' he isn't exactly sure about Hannah and me being together. He threatened me but good first time we met, and that was afore I knew who he was."

There was a sudden pounding behind them. Back at the tire pile behind the barn where they'd started, someone was flipping a tire in their direction—double time. The puff of dirt from each flip's landing didn't have a chance to settle before the next flip smacked down.

"Holy shit!" Anton's return from the far end of the yard had caught him up to Ricardo's outbound progress before he'd noticed the fast pounding from the start of the yard. Sweat was streaming off Anton's face and down his chest.

They finally stopped to watch as the flipping tire approached them, continuing to mask the flipper in the cloud of raised dirt.

"Hi, boys," Colonel Gibson appeared out of the cloud as he flipped his tire past them. Ten more turns to the end of the yard, then five more until he was back beside them.

Ricardo's muscles burned just from watching him.

"Thanks. Been a while since I thought to do this," Gibson let the last flip smack down into the dirt.

Ricardo stared at where it had landed just inches from his and Anton's toes. Neither of them had sufficient self-preservation instincts God gave a mouse.

"Feels good, doesn't it?" Gibson still wore his shirt and didn't even have the decency to wipe at his brow.

"Yes sir," was all any of them could come up with.

Rather than saying anything more, Gibson flipped his tire sideways to get around them and then shifted back to continue toward the tire stack.

"Well don't that beat all," Jesse mopped his brow. He'd left his cowboy hat back where they'd started.

Gibson was at least a decade older than any of them and also the shortest by a couple inches.

"He could totally dust our asses," Anton observed quietly.

"All three of us at once, without breaking a sweat," Ricardo agreed.

"Man is a wonder," Jesse sat down on his tire.

"What do you think that's about, other than showing us all what sorry excuses we are?"

"Maybe he just was looking for a good workout," was Jesse's two cents, which wouldn't buy two parts of a nickel.

Ricardo didn't believe it. Nope, not for a second.

He heaved his tire upright and gave it a half-twist on its treads so that he could roll it back and catch up with Gibson before he left. However, the tire rolled over a prairie dog hill and flopped over sideways. When Ricardo looked up, Gibson's tire was back where it started and, except for a lingering puff of dirt, the man might never have been there.

But he felt sure that the colonel hadn't come by idly…and that it wasn't Jesse he was checking up on. Jesse and Anton had been pilots, only he himself had been a Unit operator. Of the three of them, only he had served under Colonel Gibson's command.

Had the colonel come down to watch him training? To see if he was strong enough to serve in whatever the hell Shadow Force: Psi was going to be with two civilian women aboard?

Or…

Shit!

:What's wrong?: Michelle responded immediately.

:Nothing! Didn't mean to broadcast. Sorry.:

:Tell me anyway.:

Ricardo bent down to flip his tire back toward the start point. He no longer cared that Anton had made it another ten or so flips down the yard and back more than he had.

:Manella. (Grr!):

He grunted the tire over another time. *:Just got a visit from the colonel.:*

:Got one myself from that Emily woman.:

:What did she want?:

:You first.: He could feel Michelle's silence almost as clearly as he could hear her voice. Yeah, she wouldn't say a thing until he'd explained.

:Bastard wants to know if I'm fit for service.:

:You look very fit to me.:

:I meant fit for the team. Can I be trusted?: Regrettably Ricardo already knew the answer to that one.

:Can you?:

:Go to hell, woman.:

:(Tease).:

:Little late on that.:

:Besides, I didn't go the first time you told me to. What makes you think I would this time?:

Ricardo could imagine the sweet and light tone even if he couldn't hear it. Gods but she could twist him up.

:Besides, I was distracted. As I said, you look very, very (many exclamation points) fit.:

Ricardo grunted the tire over one last time, flopping it next to Gibson's. Then he looked up as he tugged his shirt out of the back of his belt and mopped his face with it.

Michelle was perched like a cowgirl atop Gibson's flopped-down tire. She sat to one side, with her bright blue cowgirl boots resting on the other. Her button-down shirt, which she wore with the tails tied over her flat abs, matched her boots and contrasted with a pair of denim short-short cutoffs that hid only a little more than her bathing suit had. Somewhere she'd found a pink cowgirl hat with a silver medallion hatband.

:Christ, Michelle. You look unbelievable.:

:Believe it, mister.:

:What's the occasion?:

At that she shrugged uncomfortably and blushed a little.

Ricardo looked back over his shoulder. Anton was showing Jesse more tire-flipping techniques—probably some cool trick Ricardo didn't even know.

What could make her blush like that? Jesse was gone on Hannah and Anton was Michelle's semi-brother. Not like either of those men could be of interest to her.

The only other person here was…he looked down… himself. *Most beautiful damn woman in the world is blushing like that because of me?* Didn't make any damn sense because…

:Michelle?:

At her silence, he spun from Anton and Jesse to see if she too had evaporated.

She was still there.

Except her pale skin had gone true white and her eyes were so wide she could have played the terrified babe in a slasher flick.

:You okay?:

She nodded a couple of times hastily, almost losing her hat. She cleared her throat, but didn't speak aloud. *:For once, Manella, could you tell me what you're thinking? What you're really thinking?:*

:Not my first choice.:

:Tough patooties!:

:You're so cute when you try to swear.:

She shot back an impressive stream of vitriol—acid enough to make any man wilt.

:Nice.:

Now her narrowed eyes might have become burning blue lasers.

:Meant it as a compliment.: "The truth?" he asked aloud.

"The truth."

He heard the tires thumping in their direction. One flopped down to either side of him, and both Anton and Jesse offered loud whooshing noises and laughter at the workout. One of them slapped his shoulder, but he didn't look up to see which. Instead he just watched Michelle watch him.

:The truth is, I know I could never deserve a woman like you.:

:You goddamn idiot. I oughta kick your ass as hard as your sister kicked mine.: So Isobel actually had kicked Michelle.

:But...:

"Hey, you two doing that telepathy shit?" Anton leaned right down in his face. "You better not be talking dirty to my semi-sister."

:But?: Michelle prompted.

"He always goes all cute and fuzzy, like a bullfrog staring up into a flashlight whenever they're doin' their thing."

:But,: Ricardo leaned to look around Anton and concentrated on Michelle. It would probably send her running in the other direction, but he was past his ability to keep it in. *:It doesn't stop me from wanting you more than any woman I've ever met in my life.:*

"Look, Jesse. They're definitely doing that shit. You ever seen him look a woman in the eye other than when he's talking to her in his head?"

"I'd say you're right, Anton," Jesse retrieved his hat and tugged it on. "And I'm guessing that less'n you want your snoot shortened some, you might want to back off and leave them to it."

"Oh, I don't know about that. Why he's no bigger'n a flea and I could…"

But Ricardo wasn't watching him, or Jesse. He was watching Michelle…and his own reaction.

He wasn't turning and running.

He wasn't regretting his words.

For nine months, she'd been the angel in his head. Over the last three months since, he'd learned that she was even more incredible in real life. When Isobel had told him about Michelle becoming a paramedic because of what *he* had gone through, it only added to the image.

Well, his cards were on the table and he wasn't going to be the first one to flinch. He'd done that too many times over the last year. Michelle calling him a coward after he'd abandoned her at the swimming hole yesterday only emphasized that. Turning him into a coward would have only pleased those bastards in the jungle. Well, screw that shit.

Though facing Michelle was harder than facing the entire command review board at the end of the month-long Delta Force Selection Process, he didn't look away.

SHE PUSHED to her feet and stepped out of the center of Gibson's tire. Stepping up on the side of Ricardo's tire, she was briefly taller than Anton.

Not bothering to speak, she pushed her semi-brother aside as she stepped down into the middle of Ricardo's tire.

Anton stumbled backward, tripped on the edge of the tire he'd been working with, and planted his butt in the middle like he was inner tubing down a dirt river.

"Could say I warned ya some," Jesse laughed at Anton.

But neither she nor Ricardo looked aside.

Or laughed.

Now only the arc of one side of the big tire separated her from Ricardo.

His torture scars weren't confined to his back. Or maybe the ones on his chest had been in the service of Delta.

But his back.

When he'd turned to face Anton and Jesse, she'd finally seen just what they'd done to him. Long lines of scar tissue crisscrossed like a broad lacework pattern. Scars overlaid scars. She'd only had a glimpse before he'd turned back to her…too fast for her to mask her horror.

Emily had been right; it was a miracle that Ricardo had somehow regained his fighting core. How amazing did a man have to be in order to do that?

And still he watched her with his dark, unblinking gaze.

She almost asked if he was going to run, but she didn't think calling a man like Ricardo a coward twice in as many days would end well.

"You two doin' it or not? We outta rig you with some lights, like blinking deer antlers or something, to tell us when y'all are communicating," Anton commented from where he still sat in the dirt.

"They're communicating all right, just not with you," Jesse observed.

Michelle had a lifetime's practice ignoring her semi-brother and now was no different.

Unsure how to read Ricardo when he wasn't even thinking aloud, she was left having to read herself. What did she want from this moment?

That was an easy question.

She propped one foot up on the tire, rested a hand on the warm skin of his chest so that she could lean close without falling forward, and kissed him.

Ricardo didn't react; didn't kiss her back. Instead he continued to watch her—his dark eyes narrowed.

Heat flashed to her cheeks. How had she been so wrong?

As she started to pull back, Ricardo groaned. It was soft, so quiet that it might have been only in her head, but it was there.

He grabbed at the wrist of the hand she'd rested against that dusty chest, his muscles rippling beneath her fingertips. While his grip wasn't too tight, it was so solid that she knew he could do anything to her with that simple handhold. It was the same wrist he'd grabbed two days ago and she could feel how his grip mimicked the exact placement of every finger.

All he did this time was keep her in place. Not just her hand, but by the angle of his grip, she couldn't move her forearm, or even shift her body away.

For one more moment, he kissed her as gently as he might if she really was an angel. Then he snagged his other arm around her waist and crushed her against his chest. Her free arm slid around his shoulder and over his scars, but neither of them cared.

Anton made some noise in the far distance. So soft on her awareness that he might have been a mile away rather than lying at their feet.

:God damn, woman.: Ricardo's voice was tonally flat in her head as always.

59

:I'm taking that as a compliment, not a curse.:
:Shit, yeah!:
She added the exclamation point herself.
Shit, yeah, indeed!

CHAPTER 6

"Then he just kissed my semi-sister like we weren't even there," Anton was railing to Hannah as they sat aboard the small jet that was flying them eastward from Montana.

Ricardo considered the consequences of pushing Anton out the hatch at thirty-five thousand feet without a parachute, but couldn't justify the risk of depressurizing the plane and killing everybody else just for the satisfaction. Besides, the sun had set as they'd taken off. He wouldn't have the satisfaction of watching Anton fall for seven miles. Out here in the Plains states, there were barely even any city lights to help.

Instead of tossing Anton out, Ricardo was stuck sitting toe-to-toe with him in the little Gulfstream C-37A jet. Across the aisle, Jesse and Hannah sat opposite each other, with Isobel and Michelle in the pair of chairs behind him. The other eight seats were empty.

"I thought they were gonna do it right there in front of us. Didn't you, Jesse?"

Jesse glanced over at Hannah before tugging down on the brim of his hat just enough to make it hard to see his eyes.

"I think I'll give this whole discussion a pass, pardner. You want to tick off your semi-sister, I guess that's okay by me. But it doesn't strike me as the safest ride at the rodeo."

"Wimp."

"I wasn't the one whose ass ended up in the dust."

Anton started explaining to Hannah, the only one of the four seated at the very front who hadn't been there, "I just tripped, is all."

:He does go on,: Michelle sent forward. Her position placed them back to back, less than a meter apart. He could feel her there. Could feel the heat of her and it had awoken something inside him that he'd thought was dead.

:His life expectancy is dropping rapidly,: Ricardo replied. Michelle had touched him as if it was the most natural thing, as if he wasn't a horrifying mass of scars and destruction. Her hand had slid across his back like he was still human.

:Just think about that kiss, then think about the fact that he isn't getting any from anyone.:

Think about that kiss? *Even Wonder Woman couldn't have a kiss with the power of that one. :He doesn't have a girl? Why not?:*

:Ask him.:

:My guess, he keeps pissing them off.:

:Ha! Like you don't (majorly strong query)?:

"Goddamn it, Jesse. They're doing it again. Necking with their brains."

"Yep, seem to be." Jesse was definitely Texan, trying to be agreeable with everyone.

:Anton never struck me as the jealous type.:

:Oh, he's not. But in the past he has offered to murder anyone who so much as touched me.:

:Uh, he's over that now, right (amused but desperate-sounding query)?:

"Hey, semi-brother," Michelle called out over the muted roar of the jet's engines.

"What do you want, Missy?"

"What happened to your offer to kill anyone who so much as laid a finger on me?"

"Huh!" Anton grunted out, then looked across at him. "Sorry, buddy. Hate to do it, but I'm going to have to put you down like the little weasel you are for kissing my semi-sister."

"Bummer. *Thanks so much.*"

:(Giggling happily).:

"And here we all were thinking it was just the beginning of a beautiful friendship," Jesse quipped.

"Thought you were staying out of this." Hannah slapped down on the brim of Jesse's cowboy hat, forcing him to push it back up before he continued.

"If you can tell me what *this* is, I'd be more than happy to stay out of it. Why, just a month back, I was no more than an innocent flyboy for the 160th SOAR. Now we're flying to God alone knows where, with neither a hoot nor a holler about where we're headed."

Ricardo grimaced.

As soon as the location shoot was done, Isobel had been given a week off while the operation filmed lesser characters and other B-roll that they needed from the ranch. Next week they'd be shooting in a period log cabin somewhere in Idaho.

"While you're all on hiatus," Colonel Gibson had found them within minutes of the last clap-board snapping out the end of filming, "I thought you might enjoy a little trip."

The sun had set by the time the ranch helo delivered them to the Great Falls airport where the sleek little Army Gulfstream jet had been waiting for them.

Jesse and Anton had been so busy being gobsmacked that

Major Mark Henderson (retired) was their pilot, that no one realized what was going on until it was too late.

Only after they were aloft in the jet did they figure out that Gibson had led each member of the team to think that he'd given clear instructions to one of the others of Shadow Force. He'd actually given no instructions at all.

Ricardo had to admire that, even if he didn't appreciate it. The man was a master tactician in ways that Ricardo could never match.

:Any theories?:

:About what? Where Gibson is sending us or about why you're such a jerk?:

:What (question exclamation).:

:Jerk (double, triple exclamation).:

:Still, what (question). Why am I a jerk?:

"Isobel," he could hear Michelle's voice easily over the well-muffled engine noise. "If a man gave you a steamy kiss hot enough to be dialing 911, then doesn't try to get another, what would you call him?"

"Sad," Jesse whispered at him.

"Dog meat," Anton didn't try to hide his assessment. "'Course, you'd be dead if you did try."

"I would call him a jerk," Isobel said serenely.

"And if hasn't even mentioned liking it?"

Whoops.

His sister sighed loudly, "Then I would have to say that he's my brother."

Under the cover of everyone's laughter, he sent, *:I didn't want to be pushy.:*

:There's not pushy and then there's comatose.:

∽

IN THE SILENCE THAT FOLLOWED, Michelle wondered if she'd gone too far.

The silence between them stretched long enough for the other's laughter to fade and take up another conversation.

Damn it! Damn it! Damn it! She couldn't seem to help screwing up around Ricardo. They needed to be on a much louder plane and not have telepathy. Then they couldn't talk and she could maybe keep her foot our of her mouth for ten seconds in a row.

She had to be so careful around Ricardo and she kept screwing up. He'd been in a medically-induced coma for three weeks as part of saving his life, and he almost hadn't come out of it.

Forbidden to go to him, she'd spent her time in Isobel's apartment. Except when Isobel forged through her brother's prohibition against visitors, the two of them had simply huddled in the same apartment together—only rarely speaking but both taking comfort from it. Isobel dithered over choosing her next script and Michelle lost herself in the EMT courses.

For nine months, they'd lived together for the first time in the decade since college.

Not once had they spoken of Ricardo beyond his present condition; it was as if neither of them had dared. Michelle had moved out the week before he was released, careful to leave no trace of her presence in Isobel's guest bedroom.

Michelle looked at Isobel, but she was looking at something beyond Michelle's shoulder.

It was all the warning she had before Ricardo pressed the release on her seatbelt and hauled her to her feet.

:Hey!:

He ignored her protests and led her by the hand to the rearmost seats. She glanced back, but her view of the others' expressions was blocked by Isobel moving forward to join them in Ricardo's vacated seat.

:Ricardo! What the hell?:

He pushed her down into one of the only side-by-side seats, the last pair at the back of the plane. When she didn't snap her belt buckle, he reached across and did it for her before latching his own.

"What happened to the 'yourself first' rule?"

"That's oxygen masks."

"Same. Same."

"Does everything have to be a challenge with you?"

"No," at least she didn't think it did.

Ricardo didn't say a word.

She waited until she couldn't stand the silence any longer, *:I'm sorry.:*

:For what?:

:For the comatose remark.:

:Seriously.:

Michelle wanted to bury her face in her hands. The churn in her gut had her looking around for the nearest barf bag.

He remained stonily silent; his hands clasped tightly in front of him.

:I'm so sorry. Please forgive me.: The last sounded like a wail in her head. That one moment had been so good and she'd screwed it up so badly that—

:I meant it like, Seriously (question mark). You think I don't know that I was tortured or comatose or any of the rest of it (query). Could wish that you didn't know, but that ship already sailed.:

"Can we just talk? Out loud?" Her gut still twisted in such a painful knot that she wasn't sure about whether or not it was safe to breathe.

"You first."

"I don't seem to be having much success with that." When

he didn't start, she reached out. *:Please. (begging shamelessly) (or shamefacedly).:*

:I...: Ricardo forced himself to speak aloud. "I already talk more to you than I do to anybody."

"Not Isobel."

"Okay, maybe not...but maybe. Are you jealous of my sister?"

"Yes!" *:Oh God, don't tell her I said that.:*

"Like she wouldn't already know. Remember what she can do."

Michelle glanced forward. If Isobel was aware of Michelle's feelings, she wasn't making any sign.

Anton's laugh rolled down the plane. He held out a palm and Isobel high-fived it.

Please let that not be about her.

"You're jealous of Isobel because I speak to her? She's my twin."

"Maybe jealous is the wrong word. Envious?"

"Of what?"

:I wish I'd never said anything.:

:Too late. Give, Bowman.:

Michelle wished she was braver than she knew she was.

Ricardo slipped out a hand and took one of hers, lacing their fingers together.

Not trusting her thoughts, she spoke aloud. "I listened to you for six days of hell. At first, I figured you weren't real. I thought you were just a scary-as-shit nightmare. For six days it was, from our mental breakthrough until Anton saved you."

"Wouldn't have made it through even those days if it wasn't for the hope you gave me. Took me a while to believe you were real as well. Didn't know there could be that much goodness out there." He reached out with his free hand and drew a line of fire down her cheek with a soft touch.

How could he be *so* wrong? About everything! She wasn't any of that. Desperate to not have to say that, she just blundered ahead…

"Do you remember what you were begging for the whole time?"

"To make it stop."

"No. You were begging me to tell your sister that you loved her. Nothing else. Just that."

"Oh, right." He tightened his hand in hers. "Okay then. It's just that after Daddy skipped on us and Ma had to work so hard, Isobel practically raised me. She's more my mother than Ma ever was. I went Army to help keep Izzy safe. I sent her all my paychecks to stay in college after Ma died."

"I—" But she couldn't say it.

There was just no possible way.

She wanted someone to love her that unconditionally.

She wanted…the man who could place his words in her head to love her that much.

Even if she didn't know whether she had the capacity to love him back.

CHAPTER 7

"hat the hell you up to, man?" Anton jostled him awake with an elbow to the ribs, too hard to be an accident.

Still in the plane. Still night. Scattered lights far below said they were still at cruise altitude.

"Ugh! You're an ugly mug to wake up to." Ricardo rubbed his eyes and tried to make sense of the change. He'd been holding Michelle's hand. Finally feeling at peace for the first time since forever, he'd been lulled by that ultimate sleep aid for any Spec Ops soldier, the soft roar of a jet engine prior to a mission. And he'd woken to—

"Hey! I like this ugly mug."

"I'd rather be looking at your sister's. Way prettier than you."

"Yeah, she got all the beauty and I got all the brawn. Just don't be saying that kinda shit around me, okay?"

"Why not?"

"Look, Ricardo, I get that my sister is a hot number, but she's just Missy in my head. My semi-sister or whatever she decides to call us this month. I don't need you or any other half-pint twerp messing with that."

"Trust me, I feel your pain," he nodded forward to where Isobel sat opposite Michelle. "Except I get the whole *world* telling me that about her: movie posters, sexy trailers, all of it."

"Ouch, bro. Didn't think of that. But just...lay off, you know."

"Do I still get to kiss her?"

"That something you planning on doing again?"

"Hell yeah. If she's willing, I absolutely am."

"Shit," Anton sighed deeply. "And I really liked you."

"Liked?"

"Gonna have to bust your ass up into teeny tiny pieces. Trust me, it'll hurt you more than it'll hurt me but it's still gonna hurt, 'cause, you know, you're the man, bro." Anton held up a fist, like asking for a friendly fist bump.

So Ricardo gave it to him.

Then Anton dropped his fist—about the size of Ricardo's head—back into his lap.

"Tell me how it is you two have the same parents but don't sound anything alike."

"Dude, weren't you listening none? We got no parents in common. They're—"

"You two have had the same parents since you were three, no matter who birthed you."

"But we're—"

"Yeah, *semi*-siblings, like you're a truck convoy or something. Give it up. So what's the difference? You play good old country boy to the hilt and she's—" Ricardo shrugged. He wasn't sure just what Michelle was.

"I sound like a good old country boy because that's what I am. Ma and Pa weren't nothing fancy—just North Carolina farmers. I mighta gone military, but I always wanted to be just like them. Whereas Missy…"

"Wanted to be anything else?"

Anton nodded. "Yeah. She was never content. She has a really good ear, so she'd listen to all these online video tutorial things, copy their accents. You'd never know who was gonna show up at the dinner table. French, Scottish, even this weird Yankee stuff that she said was authentic Massachusetts fisherfolk. I had to threaten her with the murder of her Smurfs collection to get rid of the California Valley girl. Ended up with this accentless thing that she says is from the Pacific Northwest."

"She doesn't sound so accentless to me." In fact, her softest Texas was music to his San Antonio-bred ears. So much so that now he heard her like that in his head as well.

"That's your fault. Goddamn it, I *am* gonna have to smush your head down to peanut sized. Oh, some of it's Isobel's fault, but that whole Texas-Latino thing she's got going is mostly your shit."

Languages had always been a bitch for him. There wasn't a Delta operator alive who couldn't wield at least two or three extras. He could learn the vocab and grammar fast enough, but getting the sound right was a real bear. Mexico and South America were the biggest pain. Every country's accent was so regional that blending in was a total bear.

"What does she sound like when she's just being her?"

"Hell if I know, man."

"But you're her brother."

"Semi-brother, yeah. And to show just how little I know, it's your sorry self she wants to be kissing."

"But she could do so much better."

Anton eyed him strangely, "You believe that shit?"

"I *know* that shit."

"Damn it!"

"What?"

"Now I really am going to have to pound your ass, Ricardo. At least hard enough to pop your head out of it. A woman like Missy comes at you, you do *not* turn her away."

"Not even to save myself an ass-whupping from her semi-brother?"

"Not even."

Ricardo glanced forward, but Michelle was hidden by the seat backs. It wasn't like she could have gotten off. She had to be here.

:Hey,: he sent up the aisle. He just wanted to see if—

:Go away.:

He waited, but that was it.

Crap!

Too bad this was an Army C-37A. It meant the galley was dry, because he'd be really happy to get drunk right at the moment.

"WHAT WAS THAT?" Isobel arched one of eyebrows at her.

"Just me telling Ricardo to go away."

"Like opposite corners of the plane isn't far enough?"

Michelle shook her head. It was nowhere near far enough.

"What do you have against my brother?"

Michelle glanced across the aisle at Hannah and Jesse, but they were both asleep—with their ankles overlapping for crying out loud. She turned back to Isobel but didn't have a good answer, so she offered a bad one, "Everything!"

Isobel laughed right in her face.

"And no, I don't need you to tell me that my feelings are mixed up worse than a ladybug hatch."

"I try never to *listen* in on my friends feelings. It is too intrusive."

"Well, that's something."

"However, if you'd like I could—"

"No!"

Again that silver-screen laugh that was so human and friendly that everyone thought it was fake, but Michelle knew was the real Isobel shining through.

"Maybe you could just tell me what Ricardo is—"

"Eww! No. Why do you think I learned how to block my awareness of other's feelings to begin with? Knowing what your twin brother's emotions are is actually very creepy."

Michelle recalled the first place Ricardo's defenses had gone was that he loved his sister like a sister. But what if…"Are his feelings that *weird?*"

"Yes, at least to a female."

"Eww!" How did she not know that about him?

"Knowing that the most important thing in his entire life is baseball? For years and years. T-ball, sandlot softball, the high school team. Girls would throw themselves at him and—"

"You're not going to tell me that he'd ignore them? He doesn't strike me as the sweet, virginal type." More like the darkly dangerous outsider—silent, but always watching.

"No. But he never cared about one of them like he did baseball. Not even when they were both busy—"

"Okay, way too much information." Michelle stared up at the plane's ceiling trying to picture something that…foreign. Her teens had been about frequent mistakes, wildly passionate, deeply heartfelt mistakes—thankfully no really horrid ones. And maybe the boys had been thinking about… She'd have to agree, "Eww!"

"Do you really want to know what Ricardo is feeling?"

"No!" Michelle covered her face with both of her hands. "Yes," she mumbled without looking up.

"Ask him."

"I can't," she kept her face covered.

"Why not?"

Michelle peeked between her fingers and, just as she feared, Isobel was smiling at her like Michelle was just as much of a mess as she thought she was.

"Well?"

"Because he kissed me."

"And it was terrible?"

"It was *amazing.* Then we're alone in the back of the plane and do you know what he does?"

"I saw. He falls asleep."

"He falls asleep," she confirmed. "Why do you think I told Anton to go and wake him up but good?"

"Because you're a frustrated bitch?"

"No, because…" Michelle dropped her hands and eyed Isobel, who was enjoying this far too much.

"Don't worry, Michelle. You're far too nice a woman to be a bitch. If you wanted to wake him up, maybe *you* should have kissed *him.*"

"I didn't think of that."

"Like I said, far too nice. There is one thing about my brother that I think you missed."

Michelle eyed Isobel carefully.

"He's shy."

"No way. I've seen him with the guys."

Isobel's shrug was eloquent.

She waited, but Isobel didn't say anything more. Instead, she leaned back in her seat and closed her eyes.

Then Michelle waited a little more.

She casually glanced around her seat and down the length of the plane.

Anton was asleep.

Ricardo's gaze met hers for an instant, then shifted aside.

She ducked back out of sight. Shy, huh? Next time she certainly would kiss him. Or smack him right in the solar plexus.

CHAPTER 8

aseball, huh (query).:
:   Ricardo was moving up the aisle behind Anton, last to disembark.

He ducked down enough to see Michelle out one of the windows. The sunrise light lit her hair with deep reds and golds. She stood at the base of the short stairway and had her face raised to the sun like a worshipper. The most—

Then he saw what was behind her.

They'd landed at Pope Field on Fort Bragg, North Carolina. The home of Delta Force. The one place on earth that he least belonged anymore.

He was going to fucking kill Gibson for sending him here.

I never signed up for this shit!

:You never signed up for baseball (confused query).:

What the hell's going on here? It was bad enough that he was losing his mind, but it seemed like now he didn't even know if he was telepathying or not.

He wanted to be away from Fort Bragg and away from Michelle.

77

Maybe he should shove Anton out of the way, storm the cockpit, and get them to deposit his ass anywhere but here. Middle of the ocean without a life raft would be an improvement—just him and a bunch of deadly sharks. He didn't care. Of course, he and Michelle had already proven that their telepathy "gift" could span thousands of miles.

With his luck, she could probably mess with his brain out to the moon. Was he too banged up to get on a Mars mission? Probably.

:Your sister said you were really big on baseball.:

:I guess. Long time ago. Kept me out of trouble.:

:You in trouble a lot?:

:It's my middle name. You were the perfect kid (not query, statement).:

:Anton must have been telling you about himself. I was, as you mentioned, a total pain in the ass.:

Last one out, Ricardo stood at the head of the steps, blinking at the dawn light and the familiar megaton humidity blast of Fort Bragg, North Carolina. Near enough to the coast to get all of the moisture and far enough away to get none of the maritime breezes tempering the heat.

He was sure he'd never sent that "Never signed up for this shit" remark to Michelle. Nor the "Pain in the ass" one, no matter how many times he'd thought it. Now he had to watch even his thoughts around her? *Damned hard not to have thoughts about her.*

Michelle was smiling at him when he finally descended the six stairs to the pavement.

Why doesn't this look good?

Her smile grew.

:You know something.:

:Many things, Manella. Too bad you'll never know what they are.:

:Heartbroken. Not.: For a distraction he looked around.

He'd been in and out of here hundreds of times over his years of Ranger and Airborne training and finally in his years walking tall for The Unit. Delta Force was as high as a man could go. Ex-Delta—you couldn't go much lower.

Everchanging, Fort Bragg seemed to never change. The teams, the training, the missions were in constant flux, but it was still itself.

Never a hot location for fighter jets, just about everything else was thick on the ground here. It was the largest US military base in the world. Transports, from the little C-12 Hurons for short range runs, and every other sized transport up to a full row of the monstrous C-5 Galaxies. There was no helo brigade based here, but there were still plenty of them buzzing around. Everything in motion yet still so familiar.

And now he was here, standing on the tarmac in a place he'd never belong again. He wasn't even Delta Force (retired) with an honorable discharge; he was ex-Delta (medically discarded). They'd given him an honorable and a medal, which basically proved he was dumb and stubborn enough to have survived—but not fit for anything else on God's green earth.

A corporal was checking each person's ID, then handing out temporary passes after noting them down on a tablet. When Ricardo handed over his Uniformed Services ID Card —with "US Army Retired" in the affiliation slot—the corporal offered him a casual salute. Once she scanned the barcode to verify Ricardo's ID, she jolted to attention and offered a much more respectful salute.

"Don't, Corporal. I'm out. You're still in the service."

She didn't ease down at all. "Heard about what you survived, Master Sergeant Manella. It's an honor."

Perfect, just what he didn't need a reminder of. *Oh, you're the poor bastard who got all fucked up in the jungle.* Forever more he'd be "Oh, that dude who had his ass tortured."

Perfect. Just perfect. But Ricardo returned the corporal's salute because it wasn't the woman's fault that his own career was gone and he had no idea what came next.

Gibson was interested in their group, like they were some shiny new toy. As if that was so much better.

A C-5 Galaxy roared aloft. America's biggest transport jet, firing hard on all four engines, blanketed the field in a shroud of silence because there was no way to speak aloud and be heard.

:That thing is huge (major capital letters on huge).: It was easy to fill in Michelle's sound of awe. Though when he glanced over, she was looking at him with a very worried expression that he wasn't going to ask about. She turned quickly to inspect the plane again.

:Yeah.: And it could be carrying thirty-six pallets of emergency relief supplies, a pair of battle tanks, or an entire Delta squadron and all of their support vehicles to go suppress a small country. He was no longer authorized to know.

:Yeah (query).:

:What?:

:What are you thinking, Manella?:

He looked over at Michelle. She stood beside Isobel, but her face was turned up to watch the massive plane punch aloft. What the hell? Why not?

:I'm thinking I don't fit anywhere anymore.:

:Idiot.:

:No argument.: The roar of the plane was tapering off. He could see a team of the 82nd Airborne jogging in formation, hustling to their flight with rifles, packs, and parachutes like they had a purpose. *Must be nice, dudes.*

"Manella!" Michelle had moved to stand toe-to-toe with him during his moment of inattention. He hated that she kept proving he'd lost his situational awareness skills. No one, absolutely no one used to be able to sneak up on him. Not even Isobel, intent on playing older sister tricks. Most of the time not even Colonel Gibson, despite his notorious skill for being stealthy.

:What?: The big jet's roar was fading into the distance and the 82nd Airborne squads were out of sight around the corner of Hangar 19. Probably just a training jump anyway, but still he envied them.

:What is wrong with you?:

As if he could answer that one. Christ, she was so close that he could smell her over the spent jet fuel and pavement heating in the morning sun—like sunshine on the surf, it just made him want to smile. Which he wasn't a bit in the mood for.

:Goddamn it, Manella.: She must actually be ticked off to make her swear.

:Everything is wrong with me. Just...leave it alone.:

She reached out and rested her fingertips on his forearm. He hadn't even been aware of crossing them over his chest. *:Okay for now. But no promises.:*

:Somehow I knew that.:

:See? You can be smart.: Then she leaned in, her breasts sliding over the backs of his folded arms, and she kissed him.

Well, that first kiss was no fluke. She tasted better than she smelled. It would be so easy to get lost in this woman.

"Cut it out, you two. We've got things to do," Anton thumped a hand down on both their shoulders, making Michelle bite the tip of his tongue in surprise. Not hard enough to draw blood, but enough to mess up a perfectly incredible kiss.

"Speaking of people who need their ass taken down," he growled up at Anton, then tested the tip of his tongue against the roof of his mouth. Yep, that was going to sting for a while.

MICHELLE MIGHT NOT BE A BITCH, but she could certainly channel "severely frustrated" easily.

She needed sleep, breakfast, and some private time with one Ricardo Manella—without her psychotic self doubts blowing up the conversation before his ridiculous conviction that he was a forevermore-failure got in the way.

What she got was a tall brunette with sun-kissed skin and a man-killer walk moseying over from a nearby helicopter like she was God's gift. Which, maybe she was. She had the kind of looks that Michelle had seen in a hundred fashion magazines—at least the really high-end ones. Except she was wearing wrap-around shades and a flightsuit instead of the latest from Vera Wang.

Anton, Ricardo, and Hannah all took one look at her and snapped to attention, offering sharp salutes.

Jesse's was more casual. "Howdy, Chief Warrant."

"Howdy yourself, Captain," the woman returned his salute first, then the others.

"They made you a Chief Warrant 4. Congratulations, Lola." He turned to the others, "This is Lola Maloney, one of Emily's best trainees." Jesse tipped his hat as he introduced her.

She punched his arm solidly, "One of? Better be checking yourself, Captain. Or is it former Captain? Heard rumors." Her accent was a lazy New Orleans; the kind that, in Michelle's experience, men tended to melt over. She'd tried the accent on for awhile in her teens, but all she'd felt was ridiculous. Better to just blend in with no accent at all.

Before Jesse could answer, Lola looked around. "And who's the other pilot?"

"That would be me, ma'am. Sergeant Anton Bowman, uh, detached."

"Detached? *Oh* but that make a girl want to ask questions that she's been ordered not to. What's your spec?"

"UH-60 Black Hawk for the 10th Mountain."

Lola leaned in close to him. "You know that Jesse is a mere AH-6 Little Bird man?"

"Some people just never measure up, ma'am, no matter what you do with them." Anton was eating up some joke that went completely over Michelle's head. She even looked up to see if her clue was flying by, but it was long gone without even waving goodbye.

"Told I'm to take three folks, though command wasn't real clear on Number Three," Lola Maloney did a sexy slouch thing and looked Ricardo up and down.

"He's mine for the day, Lola, so hands off." A short Eurasian woman strode up. She was the same five-six as Hannah but was seriously built. The only relief to her grim demeanor was a dyed streak of gold-blonde in her shoulder-length black hair. "Ricardo Manella and Hannah Tucker?"

The two of them raised their hands.

"You're with me. Kee Stevenson, Hostage Rescue Team." Her tone was short, abrupt, and had none of the friendliness or sly sexiness of the other.

This had to be better than that Lola lady.

"*The* Kee Stevenson?" Ricardo suddenly looked the way Anton had looked when Emily Beale had come up to their picnic table.

Or maybe this wasn't better. Since when did Ricardo go all goofy over a woman? He certainly hadn't done it with her.

The woman narrowed her eyes, not in mistrust, but more to say, "That was a stupid question."

"Uh, right. Sorry. I'm the Ricardo Manella one, um, person. Ah…Nice to meet you." Halfway between a salute and a handshake, he froze. When Kee didn't react to either, he dropped his hand to his side.

:What's up with you and her?:

:Nothing.:

:Bullpucky alert.:

Ricardo glanced over at her. :She's the best shooter in the military.:

:And that's a big deal (query).:

:She's probably the (major emphasis) best shooter alive today. Anywhere.:

:Still puzzled.:

Ricardo huffed out a sigh. :It's like a wannabe actress suddenly meeting my twin. Newbie, meet Isobel Manella.:

:And you're such a slouch (query). I thought Delta Force was supposed to be like the ultra-best shooters.:

:Among professional shooters, she's still Isobel. Or Meryl Streep.:

:Meryl's old. I can't believe you're hot for her.:

:Go away, Bowman.: And his attention went back to Kee, who was eyeing them strangely.

Okay, maybe they should keep the telepathy thing down to a minimum in her presence. If Anton could see them doing it, Michelle figured that meant everyone else on the planet could as well.

"I'm supposed to have a third as well," Kee said, then looked at her and Isobel.

"I'm with him!" It was out of Michelle's mouth before she even had time to think.

Isobel must have sensed it before Michelle even spoke, as she had already waved the Lola woman to move toward the helicopter and fallen in beside her.

It was a good thing that Isobel wasn't telepathic or Michelle would declare right now that she was in love with her. Isobel was the *awesomest* best friend.

"So, what are we doing?" She asked as she, Hannah, and Ricardo followed the Kee woman over to a waiting Humvee.

"Range 37," the woman said as if it was the end of a conversation, not the beginning.

Ricardo stumbled and looked at her, suddenly worried. He fell back a step and she matched him.

"You do *not* leave my side. Are we clear?" The fact that he said it aloud, even in a whisper made it all the more urgent.

"Easy, Ricardo. Goodness."

"If there's ever anything hairy going on, I'm going to expect you one step back and half a step to my left side. I'm dead serious, Michelle."

"Okay, sure." She barely swallowed a "whatever" because she didn't think that would go over well.

What in God's name was Range 37?

CHAPTER 9

"*D*on't we get breakfast first?"

Ricardo knew that questions like Michelle's only drove top trainers to push harder. It was clear that someone wanted them tired and hungry or they wouldn't have put them on a redeye flight and then taken them straight to the shooting range.

Kee Stevenson hadn't said a single word on the drive to Range 37 and now here it was. A low concrete block building, which he knew was just the locker rooms. On the far side was the armory.

Beyond that…Range 37.

It was the most intense live-fire range ever built by the military. It was as close as could be simulated to actual combat.

The trainers were relentless in keeping it realistic. When a soldier had died after trying to assault up a stairwell in Iraq, within two weeks Range 37 had an exact replica built and developed methodologies for a safe ascent before running everyone through them.

He himself had called in a new tactic used by a Mexican

drug cartel team he'd been taking down and the next time he'd gone through Range 37, he'd been confronted by that exact same scenario. He was the only one on his rotation to survive the first time through. The instructors had descended on him, unraveling his actions and then adding that to their training.

It was a hundred and thirty acres of training hell. After a year out, there was no way he was going to survive the day. And with Michelle at his side…

"Excuse me, Ms. Stevenson. Or is it sergeant?"

"Agent Stevenson. I left behind sergeant when I left SOAR."

"Roger that. Agent Stevenson, you are aware that we have a civilian with us."

"I am." She didn't break stride as she led them to the locker room building, or even bother turning to face him. "Anything else, Sergeant Manella?"

"No, just don't call me that."

She stopped and turned to face him so abruptly that he only avoided running her down by inches.

"Master Sergeant Manella," she snapped it out.

"Not anymore."

"Master Sergeant Manella. I will *not* stand by and allow you to dishonor yourself or your service by denying what you once were."

:She looks dangerous. I wouldn't mess with her, Ricardo,: Michelle chimed in.

:You're not helping.:

:I know. That's what makes me so wonderful.:

Wonderful? Definitely no comment from him at the moment.

"Look, Agent Stevenson. I don't want special treatment just because—"

"Were you or were you not an operator for Special Operations Force Delta?"

He nodded.

"Were you or were you not honorably discharged?"

"I was."

"That's all I need to know, Master Sergeant." She turned and waved him toward the men's entrance. "Full gear." Then she was gone, leading Hannah and Michelle into the other entry.

He was stripped naked and just laying out the clothes that the orderly had issued to him when Michelle chimed in.

:You never asked her about breakfast.:

:It didn't seem likely she'd pay any more attention to me than to you.:

:Well now I'm not just hungry, I'm hungry and I'm naked.:

Ricardo missed the second foot hole in his boxer shorts but snagged a toe in the elastic band. Before he could regain his balance, he tipped forward and banged his head on the locker door.

Michelle naked. No more than twenty feet away through a concrete wall.

:What are you thinking, Manella?:

Thinking? No blood in his brain for any thinking. *No! Not during training!* He couldn't afford any distractions if he was going to successfully traverse Range 37.

:Spoilsport!:

:Goddamn it! How do you always seem to know what I'm thinking?:

:Women's intuition. It's an edge we developed, oh, like half a billion years ago.:

:Half a billion years ago you were probably a trilobite.:

:My point exactly. Girl power rules. We've had it since forever.:

Ricardo didn't know why he even bothered to try.

MICHELLE WAS PRETTY PLEASED at how well she acquitted herself on the firing range. Nothing like Hannah or Ricardo, but more of Anton's shooting lessons had sunk in than she'd thought.

"You shoot decently for a civilian," Kee said in her matter of fact tone.

"Thanks," she offered back in the same tone. Maybe that was Kee's idea of high praise.

"Think less about the weapon and more about the target. Half of marksmanship is trusting your trained instincts."

"What if I don't have any trained instincts?"

Kee smiled for the first time, "Then try not to shoot any friendlies."

"No matter how tempting?" Michelle tipped her head slightly to indicate Ricardo. For the last hour all they'd been doing was simple gun handling and target practice. Well, she'd been shooting at the fifty meter targets while Ricardo and Hannah had been firing at three and five hundred meters. Yet even here Ricardo had been hovering over her like a mother hen.

"No matter how tempting," Kee confirmed.

Michelle was starting to like her.

"Shall we see what they can do?"

"Without getting me killed, if possible."

Kee pulled out a sheet of paper and handed it to Ricardo. "You have five minutes to make a plan." An armorer came and took all of their weapons, then gave ones with blue handles to both Ricardo and Hannah.

Kee took Michelle by the arm and led her toward a steel staircase that climbed the side of a building that ran all down one side of the shooting range.

"I'm not going in with them?"

Kee shook her head. "They each have ten years' experience as recon and shooters. If you were in the middle of the situation, it would defeat the entire purpose of this exercise."

"Which is?" Michelle planted herself halfway up the flight and Kee didn't resist her stopping. From here she was looking down on Ricardo and Hannah.

They were poring over the sheet Kee had given them.

To the south, the shooting range stretched out for more than a thousand yards. Beyond it stood a high berm. From even this slight vantage point, she could see a maze of dirt roads twisting across the fields beyond the berm of dirt. A convoy of trucks and armored vehicles were racing along them in tight, twisting patterns. She could see gunners firing from turrets as the vehicles rocked and bounced.

A big explosion sprayed mud aloft; some of the vehicles veered badly, then tried to get back on course. When she heard a loud thump five seconds later was when she figured out that they were a mile away.

"It's like counting lightning and thunder."

Her telepathic link with Ricardo had let them talk from San Antonio to Honduras as quickly as if sitting side by side. If their gift didn't travel at the speed of sound, did it travel at the speed of light? Or faster? Was that even possible?

Now she began to understand Colonel Gibson's orders to everyone to not ask her team any questions. If the wrong people found out about her and Ricardo's telepathy, the team would become instant lab rats. Which would totally suck.

Kee was waiting for something. To see if her attention drifted as she sent a message to Ricardo?

Wasn't gonna happen.

"So," she veered back to her original question. "What is the purpose of this exercise?"

Kee studied her intently for a moment longer before

shrugging to herself and beginning to climb the metal staircase once more.

"Ricardo and Hannah are listed as reconnaissance specialists. Ms. Tucker specialized in solo work. They need to be reminded that they are a team. At least that is Colonel Gibson's instruction."

Any other questions she might have were knocked out of her by what she found at the top of the staircase. She'd simply followed along, expecting to end up on the roof of the building for reasons unknown.

Except the building had no roof.

It had walls, doors, and windows. Dozens, perhaps hundreds of rooms were laid out before them, but no roof.

Instead, there was a massive grid of aerial catwalks that allowed people up here to walk almost anywhere above the layout.

"It's a giant shoot house," Kee waved at the expanse of interior spaces. "In here we can practice room clearing in complex interior scenarios. It's big enough that we can throw multiple twelve-person squads at it simultaneously and they'll never trip on each other. It's a chance to safely practice enemy identification and takedown in a rapid, live-fire scenario."

"Live fire like…real bullets?"

Kee didn't bother answering, instead checking her watch. "Ten seconds," she shouted down to Ricardo and Hannah.

They both nodded tersely. They already had their rifles up with the stocks propped against their shoulders, though the barrels were still aimed down and forward.

:Good luck!:

Ricardo didn't acknowledge.

Then, in an eyeblink, he and Hannah were gone in through the door.

CHAPTER 10

*S*tepping out onto the catwalk, Michelle looked down at the labyrinth of rooms the others had just entered.

Instantly, Ricardo's rifle zeroed on her for a half second, then swung away.

"Could he have—" Michelle couldn't form the rest of the words.

"Yes. I wouldn't move or speak again if I were you. Not when they're in mission mode. Though it is encouraging that he identified us as friendlies rather than shooting us."

Michelle swallowed hard but couldn't seem to breathe.

Below, Hannah hugged up close to a doorway.

Ricardo kicked it in and Hannah slid through the door.

One! Two!

Two armed targets were shot.

The only sound was the sharp spit of Hannah's silenced rifle, then the hard metal clang of the bullets hitting the target dummies.

Ricardo, a half step behind, shot them again as Hannah double-checked behind him.

He flipped both targets face down on the ground.

"Shows they're dead to any team that follows in behind them so that they don't waste a shot," Kee whispered softly enough that her voice wouldn't carry into the room below.

"But they're alone in ther—"

Kee's scowl cut her off.

Be quiet. Right.

Before it should be possible, Hannah and Ricardo flowed back out the door more like a single person than a team of two.

"Did you notice Hannah's hesitation as Ricardo shot?" Kee said softly. "She's not used to having a backup."

It had all looked like a well-oiled machine to her.

A long hallway.

A dummy leaned out from a door at the far end. It had one arm around the throat of another dummy and the other arm back to throw something. Perhaps a grenade. As Ricardo shot him twice, Hannah spun to check the hallway behind them.

They knocked down the dead dummy and leaned the innocent dummy up against a wall—one watching ahead, but the other keeping a careful eye on the dummy.

"Never know who to trust. Normally a backup team would remove the hostage."

Michelle tried to ask her question without speaking, which apparently Kee understood.

"They can't split up. Room clearing, which is what this exercise is called, as a single person is a death sentence. Probably even for people as skilled as they are. Instead, they will now have to guard front and back just in case the 'innocent' was a ruse and may now attack them from behind."

They quickly moved out of sight among the tall walls.

Kee walked away and Michelle followed. They moved well along the catwalk, then stopped again.

Michelle could hear repeated shots as the two shooters moved in their direction.

There was a small explosion and she saw a bucket dump a load of debris from the catwalk down into the maze.

"That didn't go well," Kee was smiling.

"But the shots are continuing," Michelle whispered.

"Yes. Nothing short of mortal injury will stop them. A trainer has probably marked one of them as partially disabled."

Sure enough, Michelle caught a glimpse of them several rooms away. Hannah had one arm that appeared to be tied behind her back.

"Look down."

Michelle looked.

And gasped!

"That's unfair."

"No one ever said war was fair."

Michelle considered shouting out a warning, at least to Ricardo.

"Don't distract them." Kee had turned to stare directly into her face from inches away.

Michelle bit her mental tongue, but didn't like it one bit.

Kee frowned briefly, then turned to watch below.

The room might have been a kitchen.

Three hostages sat in a line along one side of the island facing the door. Their hands were tied behind their backs, but a rifle lay on the counter in front of each one. As if they were armed.

Villains were located behind the entry door, behind a swung-open refrigerator door, and a third squatting behind the trio of hostages.

One more sat in the center of the room on a stool. His

hands were behind him as if he was bound, but he was actually holding a pair of handguns.

Michelle never could quite explain what happened next.

One moment she was staring down at a terrible, devious trap.

Then a bright flash and a loud bang had her closing her eyes in pain and slapping her hands over her ears.

When she dared open them again, all four villain dummies were down.

All three hostages were still upright.

Ricardo and the one-armed Hannah moved among them, kicking aside weapons and shooting the bad-guy dummies an extra time.

Then they paused and glanced at each other.

In that instant, someone stepped into the kitchen's doorway and shot them both.

Michelle screamed—then didn't remember anything else.

:I CAN'T BELIEVE you fainted.:

Michelle opened one eye to look at him. "You're dead."

"Only technically." Ricardo rather liked the idea that she'd fainted when she'd seen him shot.

"But I saw that man shoot you."

"It's called Simunitions."

"Like…" Michelle pushed herself up slowly, using the railing of the metal walkway to help. Then she reached out and tentatively touched his chest. He'd scaled right up the kitchen cabinets and then rushed across the thin top of the walls the moment she'd gone down.

"Like simulated ammunitions. See how most of our weapons are blue? It means they've been retrofitted for Simunitions and can't fire live rounds."

"So you're not dead."

"Well, technically we are. We dropped our guard and the trainer shot us in the backs. Got both of us." Which never, ever should have happened. He'd let his guard down for just milliseconds. Hannah was technically injured and it was his job to have her six. Instead, he'd thought about the woman up on the catwalk watching him.

He hadn't looked. He wasn't *that* far out of practice. But he'd let himself be mentally distracted in a battle scenario at just the wrong moment.

"Welcome back," Kee's tone was drier than week-old toast before she looked Ricardo in the face. "Too long out of the service."

"God damn it, Kee. You think I don't know that?" *Never should have been here in the first place, not after a year out of the service. Not ever again!*

"Doesn't matter. You were both sloppy. At corner three and room seven you both should have been injured. Swinging your rifle through the tripwire and setting off the explosion in corridor four is a trap you never should have fallen for. If you'd kept your formation tighter, you would have avoided that. Never, ever push ahead without your teammate."

"But—"

"This isn't solo recon, soldier. Keep it tight."

Nothing more useless than a broken soldier. And it hurt like a knife had been driven into his gut.

He'd lost everything of who he was.

And Michelle's look of pity didn't help a thing.

CHAPTER 11

*A*fter Hannah and Ricardo had turned in their weapons and changed back into their street clothes, the soldier who'd given them their IDs had returned. She was leading them toward a low building beside a big hangar for a briefing.

A briefing?

All Michelle could picture was like in the movies when hero pilots were all lined up in ridiculously comfortable armchairs facing some wall of big screens and speaking in cryptic messages like "Split-S" and "Go to guns."

It was weird to realize that most of her understanding of what her brother and Ricardo did came from movies like *Top Gun.* Except her brother flew helicopters rather than fighter jets and was a foot taller than Tom Cruise. And Ricardo had been a soldier for Delta Force—which was so low profile that it took the government almost forty years to admit they even existed despite a couple of low-brow 1980s Chuck Norris movies.

"Nothing more useless than a broken soldier?"

Ha!

A fashion flunky turned EMT who was a friend of a movie star. *That'll one-up you, Ricardo.*

Or one-down.

She sighed; she was in so far over her head. Maybe Colonel Gibson was right about leaving civilians like her behind.

The briefing only made that all the more true. The six of them and some intelligence officer, who never offered a name or rank. A blank room on metal chairs at three folding tables set up in a U shape. Not the least bit *Top Gun.* And without some Hollywood scriptwriter to dumb it down for her, the briefing might just as well have been in Greek. Scenarios, incursions, technology she'd never heard of…It shouldn't be possible to feel so out of place. Even Isobel appeared to be asking relevant questions and Michelle couldn't follow any of it.

:*Is this what you feel?*:

:*What?*:

:*Like you totally don't belong, not even a little?*:

Ricardo turned from the screen that hung on the wall at the head of the U of tables to look at her. The sadness in his eyes was all she had to see.

Ricardo's shrug said no, but maybe yes.

No, his shrug said to go the hell away. As if she could.

"Are there any questions?" The briefing officer looked around the table, and Michelle noticed that his eyes pretty much skipped over her. She'd tried to look attentive, but she was so out of her league and it must have been painfully obvious. Multi-unit task force, base and field security risk analysis, infiltrate-exfiltrate tactics…words, words, and more words.

:*What am I doing here?*: Michelle knew she didn't belong.

Before Ricardo could answer, the briefing officer spoke up. "I don't know what you're all doing here."

:(Laugh).:

:Go find a cliff to jump off, Manella.: She did her best to smile at him to show that it was a tease, but then the briefing officer caught her doing it and his expression went particularly dark.

"I know several of your records and I can't help but recognize Ms. Manella." The briefing officer's eyes finally skittered away from Michelle's face to focus on Isobel. Like Michelle needed even more proof that she was the misfit.

"I've been told to ask no questions. But I'm supposed to say the following: 'If you are unsure of this mission at any time, just back away.' Why I'm wasting my breath saying that to a team that includes an Army pilot, a Night Stalker, and two Delta, I have no idea. Your flight has been refueled and departs in fifteen minutes. Best of luck." Then he was gone and the corporal reappeared as their guide.

"No rest for the weary," Michelle joked as they headed back out to the refueled plane. She hadn't slept much on the flight here and the time zone had jumped ahead two hours. The coffee was battling the breakfast of fried chicken on a biscuit smothered in gravy.

And everyone else on her team all got it. Focused. Determined. Ready.

But she was—toast.

:Where are we going again (query).: She sent to Ricardo.

:Weren't you listening?:

:Gibberish quotient equals a hundred percent.: Even with the half-off, season-end discount.

Ricardo dropped into the seat at the very back of the plane. When she took a step to follow, he scowled fiercely at her for reasons she couldn't fathom. That left her no choice except to sit in the front four across from her semi-brother. Isobel rested a hand on her shoulder for a moment before trailing Ricardo all the way to the back

When Ricardo still didn't answer, she leaned forward and whispered to Anton, "Where are we going?"

"Weren't you listening?" She hated that he echoed Ricardo's question; this time she could hear the peevish disbelief.

"Just answer the damned question, Anton."

"Honduras." He didn't say it like anything special, but Michelle felt a shiver right down to her boots.

Honduras was where they'd found and rescued Ricardo.

"We can't!"

Anton shrugged. "Not like we're going back into the jungle. Just a US airbase. In and out, no problemo."

Her semi-brother was an idiot. So was she. How could she have missed that? Because she'd been too busy thinking about the changes in her and Ricardo's lives over the last year to really listen.

:Are you okay going back?: Michelle sent over her seatback.

:No!: It snapped back so hard and fast that it felt like a shout, or maybe a scream. *:Go the fuck away, Michelle. Just leave me the hell alone.: Fucking civilian.* Yeah, that's all he was anymore—a fucking, useless civilian.

Michelle cringed in her seat. Too late to get off the plane, they were already taking off. Instead, she tugged down on her pink cowboy hat and did her best to hide the tears.

It must not have worked, because Anton's big hand wrapped over where both of hers were clamped together in her lap. But still she couldn't stop.

CHAPTER 12

"*E*ven with my shields up, I felt that blast, Ricardo."

"Go to hell, sis!" He tried to match his whisper to Isobel's and nearly strangled in his attempt because his throat was so tight.

"Should I have them turn the plane around? The briefing officer said we could abort this if we got uncomfortable."

"Absolutely not! I'm not going to be some lame-ass excuse that holds the team back."

"No. You're a soldier suffering from a perfectly justifiable case of—"

"Don't say it!"

"—post-traumatic stress disorder."

"Fuck!" He so didn't need this shit. "You'll never understand, Isobel. You were never a soldier. You can't—"

"*I'll* never understand? You arrogant prick. Do you know that for the last year I haven't once closed myself off to your feelings no matter how awful they were?"

"You didn't! Not while I was..." He couldn't imagine her feeling—

"No," Isobel shook her head. "While you were being

tortured, you were too far away. Unlike you and Michelle, I need to be near someone to feel their emotions. But once you hit the Audie L. Murphy Memorial VA in San Antonio, I was able to keep my awareness with you most of the time."

"Why?"

"I didn't dare miss a second of what you were going through in case you died, you idiot. I didn't sleep at all in the first few weeks because I was afraid I'd wake up to find out you were dead. Once we knew you were going to live, I could feel how hurt you were inside. I've tried to help, but…" she raised her hands helplessly, then dropped them back into her lap.

"You did, Isobel. You were the anchor that made me fight for life. You know that, right?" When he reached out, Isobel grabbed on to his hand with both of hers.

"Nice of you to finally admit it. Do you know why I did? Because I'm your sister and I love you."

He offered her his best know-it-all half-smile, which earned him the soft laugh he'd been hoping for.

"Besides, you're one of only two people who see me as Isobel Manella, not as some movie star."

"Who's the other?"

Her single arched eyebrow, which he was pretty sure she'd practiced specifically to make him feel foolish—it worked—told him who the other person was.

"Michelle."

He didn't need her nod to confirm it.

"And you told her what I…" He couldn't imagine the horror of his emotions laid at Michelle's feet.

Isobel shook her head. "I could spare her that, at least. Though your telepathy gave her plenty to worry her."

"I don't know what to do about that. I can't turn her off."

"Is that why you just lashed out at her?"

"No." He'd done it because… Because returning to

Honduras scared the shit out of him. It was still the murder capital of the world despite the horrors in the failed states of Africa. Detroit and a few other cities were more deadly per capita, but those were cities, not entire countries.

He'd lashed out at her because…

He'd needed a target and Ms. Innocent had made a perfect one. They were flying into mortal danger and she'd been blissfully unaware.

'Where are we going again?'

Who the hell was she kidding? She was going to end up dead and somehow it was going to be his fault.

It wasn't supposed to be mortal danger—they were going to test security protocols by trying to infiltrate a secure military airbase. The worst that should happen was that they were arrested by American soldiers and the exercise would be over. They wouldn't be strolling through the guarded perimeter of a drug lord's smuggling camp.

There was almost no chance of her dying. Probably less danger than crossing the road in San Antonio.

He really *had* become a fucking civilian. In all the worst ways. Even yelling at himself hadn't made it this clear. He'd fallen out of the military in a year-long swan dive to crash land as the worst liability on a team that included two civilians more competent than he'd ever be again. So scared of his old Honduran shadow that he wanted to beg Isobel to turn the plane around to let him off.

He was worse than a fucking clueless civilian, he was a terrified one.

And he'd unleashed all of his own fears and failures on Michelle's innocent head. Worse, *inside* her head.

"I've got to—" Ricardo popped his seatbelt and headed forward.

"Don't!" Isobel called after him, but he ignored her as he headed up the aisle toward Michelle. They hadn't reached cruising altitude, so it was an uphill struggle to climb the aisle.

Anton saw him coming, rose from his seat, and blocked him two-thirds of the way there.

"Turn around, bro," Anton sounded friendly enough, but there was certainly no way to get around him.

"I just have to—"

"Only shit you have to do is turn your narrow Texan ass around and leave my sister alone." Maybe less friendly than Ricardo had thought.

"I just want to—"

"Now!"

"I—" Why was he trying to argue with Anton? *:I'm sorry, Michelle. I don't know why I did that.:*

The top of her hat shifted, showing that she was awake, but she didn't reply or turn to look at him.

Ricardo's head banged against the low ceiling as Anton lifted him off his feet by a massive hand clamped around Ricardo's throat.

"What part of 'leave my sister alone' didn't you understand?"

Ricardo knew any number of techniques to break free, except when his attacker was also a friend.

"I—" he managed to squeak out.

"Enough of your whining, Manella. She's eaten your shit for a year and it's the last goddamn time. Now stop being the fucking victim and get back to your seat before I open a door and toss you out for the sharks to feed on." Anton heaved him backward, thankfully in line with the aisle. Ricardo tumbled through a backward somersault to collapse prostrate at Isobel's feet.

Anton scowled at him for a long moment before returning to his seat at the front of the plane.

"I tried to warn you," Isobel looked down at him.

"Since when was I ever smart enough to follow your advice?" Christ but his throat hurt.

"Since never," Isobel bent over to pat his cheek.

Ricardo clambered once more into his seat and waited for the plane to quiet.

He knew it was stupid, so rather than asking Isobel's advice, he tried again anyway.

:Michelle?:

Silence.

CHAPTER 13

*T*hree hours and no sleep later, they were starting the long descent into Honduras.

"Ricardo or I could walk into Soto Cano Air Base with no one the wiser." Hannah Tucker had called the meeting before Michelle could figure out how to hide in an airplane cabin forty-five feet long, seven wide, and six high.

Hannah had called them all to the center seating area of the plane, a couch for three along one side, two chairs across the aisle, and Ricardo hovering in the aisle at the far end of the group.

Anton had rolled out a map across his and Michelle's knees, but she couldn't make much sense of it. A runway, some big buildings, some small buildings, and a town beyond that.

With Isobel sitting by Ricardo, she couldn't go to her friend. Anton offered sympathy and had kept Ricardo away, but that wasn't what she really needed.

What she really needed?

As if she had any idea what that was.

For a year she'd been scrabbling around in search of

having some purpose or meaning in life. No longer able to tolerate her past self, she was no closer to finding her new self. She could now see that hiding in her EMT studies had achieved nothing beyond chewing up most of her thinking time over the last year.

It's not like she'd rushed out to get a job even though there was a huge demand out there. She hadn't been top-of-the-class, but she'd been close enough that offers came in without her asking. Seattle sounded good. Or Boston. Those were the two farthest from San Antonio. But her semi-brother and her best friend lived in San Antonio. This sucked in so many spectacular ways.

And now that she had time to think, she couldn't seem to put even two words together. Except "sad" and "ridiculous." She'd put those two together just fine.

Her parents had spent a lifetime telling her that she was "different" and "sure didn't fit in 'round these parts." As if she didn't know what a misfit she was. Anton had joined Junior ROTC in high school and missed his own graduation because he was due at bootcamp. He'd always had a calling and she'd…

"But that isn't a decent test of base security," Hannah was still speaking. "By command's lack of instruction, and intentionally sending us in with no guidance and too little sleep, I think they're hoping to see what we can do that they don't expect. This isn't just a test of the base, it's a test of us. So, who has an out-of-the-box idea?"

"Two teams. Boys and girls," Michelle spoke up right away. That way she wouldn't end up on the same team as Ricardo no matter what happened.

Isobel tipped her head in thought. Of course she'd know Michelle's motivation, be able to read it on her face even if she wasn't sensing Michelle's emotions. Four years as college roommates and then living together during the first nine months of Ricardo's recovery didn't allow for many secrets. But neither did she dismiss it out of hand.

"Interesting," was Hannah's comment as she also tested the idea. "How?"

How? "Uh…Isobel is injured. I'm an EMT. They said that one of the principle missions of the US force in Honduras was medical outreach. We throw ourselves on their mercy as innocent civilians and then attack from the hospital or whatever." She was actually pretty impressed with herself. She must have picked up more at the briefing than she'd expected. Or maybe it was from watching too many movies.

"How do you arrive? A car or what? Certainly not in a US Army jet with a pair of Army pilots."

"A helicopter," Anton spoke up. "We land at the capital's airport. Hire or swipe a helo, then come in fast and low on the Soto Cano Airbase."

Jesse tipped back his cowboy hat. "And get our behinds shot out from the sky. Nope, come in on the emergency frequency just like normal folks in trouble."

"But none of us girls fly helicopters," Michelle still liked her first idea.

"I'd be right glad to pitch for the other team," Jesse tipped his hat to her.

Jesse was a Night Stalker. Isobel, Jesse, and herself? She could deal with that.

Ricardo was staring at her, but he didn't speak—not aloud, not in her head, and not even one of those internal dialog things. Isobel had said to ask him what he was feeling. Well, she knew what he was feeling, loud and clear, without asking—*fucking civilian.* Like she was lower than dirt. Well, she already knew that.

Let's see him figure out as neat a way in.

Ricardo glanced at Anton and Hannah. "We three all speak Spanish?"

The others nodded.

"How about this? We're going in on a surprise inspection of the Honduran Air Force Training Base that's adjacent to Joint Task Force-Bravo's section of the base. We'll liberate a Humvee or a Jeep."

Good. Two separate attacks. Nothing to do with each other.

"No radio traffic." Then he looked directly at her for the first time. *:Sorry. But we'd be foolish to not use our gift.:*

Michelle tried to meet his steady gaze, but couldn't and had to look away.

She hated that he was right. Too bad it wasn't a gift— more like a plague.

CHAPTER 14

*R*icardo sat in the back booth at the Cafetería Maravilla and wished he was drinking a Port Royal lager. Hell, he'd even take a lame, watery Barena. But he was on duty, and alcohol didn't mix well with a military operation—even if he wasn't military anymore. So, he sat drinking ice water and watching the room.

The Maravilla sat just outside the fence from the Honduran Air Force Academy, which was the only thing to recommend it. A standard, one-story hole-in-the-wall except it was built on a scale big enough to take on the rowdiness of several classes of the academy's cadets. They were clustered up front where they could get first dibs on any women dumb or desperate enough to come here to find a good a time.

Down the far side of the bar were several clusters of the more serious drinkers—contractors for the US side of the base. The 1st Battalion, 228th Aviation Regiment and all the other units of Joint Task Force-Bravo had been stationed here for most of the last forty years. They'd built up a presence of several hundred contractors, including maintenance and training personnel—and security.

Ricardo found what he was looking for at the third table from the back.

A trio of guys who were dressed quasi-military, just too cool for the world. Army boots, camo pants, and too-tight black t-shirts that showed off their muscles. But it wasn't the $300 mirrored Ray-Ban aviators that they still wore, even though the inside of the Maravilla was dark even at midafternoon, that tipped Ricardo off.

It was the attitude.

Military, who hadn't trained on how to blend in like a Delta operator, often had a swagger. But this trio had a swagger like they were God's gift on two legs. Too obvious about scanning the room, but not one had picked him out— they were obviously scanning to see how others were "admiring" them. Mercenaries for hire.

When their leader headed for the toilet, Ricardo rose casually and entered first—he'd chosen a table close by the entry.

Mr. Hotshot went up to a urinal.

Ricardo chopped him hard and he dropped to the cracked white tile like a sack of rotten potatoes. It only took a moment to drag him into one of the stalls, drop his pants around his ankles, and lock the stall door.

Bingo! He had an electronic key in his pocket. It would make it easy to identify his vehicle, even if Hannah out in the parking lot hadn't spotted which was which. He pulled the guy's ID—the two of them looked a little alike—and his cash while he was at it.

"Nice glasses, dude. Bet I'd look good in them," Ricardo pulled them on.

He didn't even have to crawl out. The old metal dividers were so worn, probably by Honduran cadets with a lousy idea of where to show a woman a good time—*up against a men's stall wasn't it, guys*—that he could flex the frame panels open without unlocking the door. After he slipped out, it was easy to flex it once more and lock Mr. Hotshot's door from the outside. Anyone looking for him would see his pants around his ankles under the door and leave him alone for a while.

They only needed a few minutes' head start anyway.

He dropped all of the guy's five-hundred-lempira notes by his own water glass. Each bill was only twenty bucks US, but the wad would make up for what a shitty tipper the guy probably was.

Out in the parking lot, he spotted Hannah and Anton leaning against the front bumper of a Humvee as if they were just enjoying the scorching sun. Sure enough, when he hit the button on the electronic key, the Humvee chirped, surprising Anton enough to jump away.

"Nice glasses," was all Hannah said before heading for the driver's door.

With a shrug he took shotgun, leaving Anton to take a back seat. Humvees were designed to seat four soldiers in full battle kit, so Anton fit just fine in the back.

"Hey, these dudes have some pretty, hard-shell cases back here," Anton remarked after he climbed in. "Did you get a key?"

Ricardo tossed the fob and attached keys back over his shoulder. It only took Anton a moment to unlock whatever he'd found.

Hannah rolled them out of the parking lot. He caught her slight head motion to check the rearview mirrors. She didn't check again. No action from Mr. Hotshot's buddies. They'd rolled out clean.

Yeah! Something you so didn't do with Michelle, dude. He hadn't done that clean at all. He'd buggered it all up bigtime.

The woman had fainted over him being shot.

And then he'd told her to fuck off because he couldn't deal with going back into Honduras.

Didn't seem like she was going to be letting him undo it anytime soon, either. Be better for her if she didn't anyway, which would suck for him. Which described most of his last year. Except for winding up dead, it would be hard to have a worse year. Yeah, just like Delta had taught him, sometimes you just had to embrace the suck. He had that trick down.

"Let's see," the snap of latches from the back. "A matching set of very pretty M4A1 rifles. Decent set of night optics. Underslung grenade launchers." Another case's locks snicked open. "Glock 22s with enough magazines to rob half the banks between here and Tuscaloosa. Ooo, thermite grenades. What fun." Then Anton let out a low whistle of surprise.

Ricardo was just turning to see what Anton had found when a fat bundle of money dropped into his lap. Not Honduran lempira—US currency. Ricardo fanned the bundle —nonsequential hundred-dollar bills.

"Nice. Got more of those?"

A fistful of bundles dropped over his shoulder, and with Anton's fist, that was a whole lot of money. "Bundles of a hundred makes each ten grand. I got at least fifty of them back here."

Hannah glanced over at him, then turned back to the road.

Drive on by? would be her unspoken question.

Abort the mission and don't even turn in was the sensible option. This wasn't just some security contractor's Humvee they'd carjacked for a few hours. Not with an onboard armory and a half million in hard cash sitting in the back. They'd just stepped into some kind of shit it was better not to know about.

"Here's another caseful o' cash," Anton announced merrily.

A million. Far safer to abort, dump the vehicle, and go for another. Not just bad news. These guys were going to come hunting for whoever had jacked their vehicle and they were going to come hard.

Oddly, that made being on the base the safest place. There they'd be surrounded by the very forces they were here to fool.

Just then a civilian Bell LongRanger swooped by overhead. He watched it for the space of three heartbeats as it turned for final approach to the airfield. No need to bother Michelle and ask if that was their team. Only a Night Stalker would fly that way. He'd ridden enough deep insertions in their aircraft to recognize Jesse's perfect control.

"They're already in," he told Hannah.

Rather than bypassing the gate, she turned in and they were committed.

Ricardo handed all except one bundle of cash back to Anton.

Now it was going to get interesting.

"I DO NOT LIKE THE BLOOD!" Isobel said for about the hundredth time.

"Wimp! Besides, you still look amazing. Bet you'd even make a lovely corpse." Michelle had her hooked up to a saline drip, because who didn't get dehydrated in Honduras' oppressive heat? Blood pressure cuff. Half a dozen bandages, as if for scattered cuts and scrapes. Several of them bloodied with a bag of blood they'd bought at a butcher's shop in Tegucigalpa.

"But I liked these jeans."

"Five-hundred-dollar Calvin Kleins?" They so weren't.

"Forty-nine at Walmart. I still think like the girl who grew up poor."

"Good." Because Michelle had felt a little guilty about cutting the big slice across the thigh. "Maybe we'll make them into cutoffs afterward."

"You just stay away from me with your scissors."

"I have shears and scalpels, but no scissors." Thankfully she'd had her EMT med kit with her and hadn't needed to fake anything except the blood.

"Jesse, could you rescue me from this woman?" Isobel called out.

"He can't hear you. He's too busy talking to the tower and getting us on the ground."

"We're here already?"

"Yes, the Army medics of Soto Cano Air Base eagerly await your arrival. So get ready to put on your best, oh-so-helpless-movie-star-who-fell-down-a-cliff-while-on-an-outing-from-a-cruise-ship act."

"Oh, yes. How did I do that again?"

"By being an airheaded idiot."

Isobel scowled at her. "You're enjoying this."

"Must say I am."

Isobel lay back with a sigh. "I guess I should have expected this."

"What?" Michelle glanced out the window and saw that the ground was close. A team waited with a rolling gurney ready to whisk Isobel into emergency care. She checked body temperature, oxygenation, and blood pressure again just to be ready with the vitals report any decent EMT would deliver with the patient. "You're far too healthy."

"I should have expected you'd take out your anger at Ricardo on me."

"Oh, I'd never do that to you," Michelle whispered fast as

she repacked her gear bag. The skids touched down on the pavement.

The cargo door was whisked aside and suddenly three male orderlies were easing Isobel's stretcher out the door and onto the gurney.

"No," she told the empty cargo bay before climbing down to follow along. "Ricardo will get *all* of what's coming to him himself."

CHAPTER 15

"*I*Ds please."

Ricardo passed the stolen Security Teams International's card to Hannah, along with the CAC (Common Access Card). He hesitated a moment to see who he was supposed to be, should have read them sooner. He was Jack Harper, a former Green Beret Sergeant E-5.

Lame, dude. Ten years in and didn't make staff sergeant. Well, Ricardo knew enough to read between the lines that the guy had been eased out, without doing anything so heinous as to be tossed out. It certainly would explain the guy's bruised ego.

Ricardo was careful to keep his face in the Humvee's internal shadows. If the guy was properly trained, he'd pull a flashlight to check his face. Ricardo might be able to pull it off with the sunglasses, but…

Nope. Guy didn't even try.

"May I have the other IDs please."

Regular forces. Last name on his jacket: Jeffries.

"They're with me, Jeffries. Better not to ask questions."

"Uh…" the soldier hesitated for a long moment.

Anton passed forward a Glock 22 in a shoulder harness. Ricardo made a show of shrugging it on. Once he was settled, he slid his stolen sunglasses just far enough down his nose to glare at the guard. The glasses would now shade his cheekbones as he leaned partway into the sunlight coming in through the windshield. It was okay, the corporal wouldn't think to look at the ID again.

Jeffries had start-of-first-foreign-tour written all over him. No one else looked so neat and precise at a foreign airbase. A bribe attempt might get them shot—the kid would still be too straitlaced to try that ploy. But a strong-arm tactic would cow him under unless he was well above the average lot.

"Best not to ask, Jeffries. Some things you really don't want to know." He pushed up his sunglasses, leaned back into the shade, and waved a hand for Jeffries to lift the barrier.

Another hesitation. Hannah played the role perfectly, kept her hands quiet on the wheel and looked straight ahead, waiting like the perfect automaton.

Finally Jeffries signed his own demotion back to private by raising the barrier and waving them through.

"Way too easy, bro," Anton announced from the back.

"You're right. But it's only Layer One. It heats up from here."

"Right or left?" Hannah asked as she slowed at the end of the short entry drive.

The airfield lay spread out before them. A pair of single propeller, Tucano trainers painted in bright camo-green were practicing touch-and-gos on the field. Their dangerous-looking outlines were blurred by the heat shimmering off the runway.

To the right lay the Honduran Air Force Academy. There was opportunity for some mayhem there. But souring the marginal relations with a ruthless and corrupt government wasn't on the agenda.

"Left."

To the left lay the section of the air base rented to the American Joint Task Force-Bravo. The 1st Battalion, 228th Aviation Regiment specialized in helo operations for security, narcotics, and post-storm search-and-rescue operations throughout Central America. A high order for less than two dozen helos—took some seriously good guys to pull that off. They were backed by logistics, support, and most importantly, medical elements. Also, in addition to contracted security, they boasted a Joint Security Force of MPs. They would be the toughest hombres to deal with.

Far down the field, he could see the cluster of people rushing a stretcher from the helo to one of the buildings.

Three big Chinook helos and a pair of Black Hawks were parked between their positions.

:Everything okay?:

:Busy! Go away!: And Michelle was gone. He could practically hear the door slam in his face.

"Missy just slap your ass down, bro?" Anton practically chortled from the back seat. "Didn't know much could make one of you silent Delta types flinch, but she's sure got your number!"

"Time to saddle up," Hannah whispered softly.

This time they'd been spotted by a security patrol. That was their route in, surprise inspection. But he had no ID to flash except—

That's when he spotted how they moved. Not regular forces. They had moves that only came from Special Forces or Special Operations training. More contractors working for Security Teams International—they'd know Jack Harper.

They'd probably know Jack Harper. Hell, they were

probably waving them over to one of the open hangars because they recognized his vehicle.

"Not good. Very not good."

EVERYTHING WAS HAPPENING TOO FAST.

The medics were rushing Isobel into the medical center. Michelle was trying to lag behind enough to give Jesse a lead to follow, but he had to finish shutting down the helicopter. She didn't want to be left behind by Isobel's medical team and risk being shut out either.

The last thing she had time for was giving Ricardo some lame status update. They were busy doing exactly what they were supposed to be doing.

A glance back as she passed through the swinging glass doors, and she saw Jesse was half out of the helo, mostly hidden on its far side. By the direction of his cowboy hat, he wasn't facing her direction, instead he was looking…

Michelle followed the direction of his hat's gaze. A Humvee was rushing up to him—with a man in the rooftop turret aiming a massive machine gun at Jesse's chest. But they'd already been cleared onto the base by security. Security who were nowhere to be seen because they were busy escorting Isobel and the doctors deeper into the building.

A large portion of EMT training was triage: identify the severity of a wide variety of patients, select action priority, and take it immediately.

The uninjured Isobel would have some explaining to do to the doctors when they removed her bandages and discovered healthy skin.

Jesse was in imminent peril.

Not even hesitating, she spun on her heel and was

striding back out the doors as fast as she'd come in through them. Only as she crossed back to the helo did it strike her that she'd just put herself in harm's way as well as Jesse. Too late to take it back as the Humvee's driver swung open his door and aimed a rifle at her.

She'd never faced a gun before. Anton had tried to teach her how to shoot, but she'd never been interested in it. Right now that seemed like a really, really stupid decision—not that she was armed with more than a medical bag.

Michelle was so sick of it all.

Never fitting in.

Never good enough.

Fucking civilian, according to Ricardo.

She was!

What was so wrong about being a civilian?

Why was it so important to fit in and conform?

And *now* they were pointing a gun at her as if she was some criminal low life?

It was too much. It was just too *damned* much!

She stalked up to the driver, who kept his gun aimed at her chest.

Some crazed part of her that she barely recognized slapped aside the rifle's barrel and she swung her gear bag off her shoulder and held it right in the driver's face.

"You see this?" Michelle shouted right in his face. She pulled it back enough that she could point at the big white cross on her red bag and the big "EMT" block-printed below it. "Do you know what this means? It means I'm medical personnel and you should leave me and my pilot the hell alone! Now back off!"

It *was* crazy. She didn't know if she'd ever been so mad in her life.

Mad at them. Mad at how her life wasn't making any

sense. Even madder than Ricardo could make her—which was *really* saying something.

He made even less reaction that Ricardo would have, which was saying something. She bit back on her temper and sought calm, which was damned hard at the moment.

"Look, officer. My pilot and I are part of a security team test." No point keeping that hidden any longer. "We're no threat. We were just sent in to test your security and I guess it was pretty good because you caught us."

The soldier remained stone-faced as he studied her through his mirrored shades for a moment. Then he slowly turned to look at his buddy.

She'd expected surprise or even anger—having someone say they didn't trust you when you were a security force probably wasn't the nicest thing.

Michelle didn't expect to see fear.

The man turned back to her.

What were they up to that they *feared* a security checkup?

She barely saw the fist that connected with her chin. Nor did she remember falling. She did hear the sound of her head hitting the pavement, but was thankfully unconscious before she felt it.

CHAPTER 16

*O*nce they'd rolled the Humvee into the hangar, the doors had been slid shut. The cool shadows were a relief from the blazing tropical sun.

The leader, who'd waved them toward the hangar, leaned his crossed arms on the rolled-down driver's window.

"Only you, Jack, would bring some babe to a drug deal." There was a laugh.

Drugs? That explained the bundles of money.

But Shadow Force was supposed to be testing for security holes, not facing down drug dealers.

Honduran drug dealers.

Again!

He felt colder than a winter's mission in the Ural Mountains.

The shadows inside the hangar masked that Ricardo wasn't Jack, but he didn't dare speak—he'd lose the few seconds of surprise he had.

Thankfully, Hannah covered for him by yanking out a handgun—that he'd never even seen her stash away—and ramming its muzzle against the underside of the leader's chin.

"Now, if you just take it easy, we'll get along fine." Her voice was Delta operator chill.

"Right, babe. Grab a clue. Tell her to chill, Jack."

Then his eyes focused on Ricardo's face and registered that he wasn't Jack Harper.

"Shit!" He slapped for his own sidearm.

Ricardo thought it better not to ask if Hannah pulled the trigger or the guy's gesture of reaching across to his own shoulder holster had slapped her hand, making her jerk the trigger. He couldn't have heard the answer anyway as the loud report of the shot echoed inside the Humvee and left his ears ringing.

The leader's brains fountained out behind him.

Ricardo rolled out the other door. As he did, he saw others in the hangar grabbing for their sidearms. He hit the floor and rolled underneath the Humvee.

Two people had closed the hangar doors. Three more had been standing behind the leader. Possibly others, but he'd been taught to deal with the targets you could see first and to worry about the others later.

He had no line on the trio as the leader's body dropped to lie on the concrete and stare blankly at him. His face looked fine—if you ignore the small entry hole under his chin—it was the back of his head that was missing.

Twisting around, Ricardo kneecapped the two still standing to the rear of the Humvee by the hangar doors. When they screamed and fell, he drilled them with another shot each to the face. He didn't dare waste another shot just to be sure they were dead—Anton hadn't given him any spare magazines. He just hoped that this one was the full fifteen rounds. In which case he still had eleven to go.

He quickly scanned what he could see between the tires and the dead bodies piling up on the floor.

Nothing doing.

He rolled up close to dead guy Number One lying below Hannah's door.

:Michelle. Abort! There's a drug deal going down here.:

Nothing.

:Michelle, goddamn it. This is real world, not time for emotion shit. Answer me.:

More nothing.

He was going to strangle that woman the next time he saw her.

A full-blown firefight was going on above him—Hannah and Anton from inside the armored Humvee versus at least three more backup men. Thankfully the windows were also bulletproof to mere rifle fire.

Two of the three men outside the driver's side of the vehicle were down by the time he snaked around the first corpse to get a line on the last man attacking from that side who, as he went down, got off a burst from his rifle. Thankfully he was set to a three-round burst rather than full automatic. Two rounds thudded into his dead leader's body, but the third found a gap between the dead guy and the bottom edge of the Humvee. A sudden fire lit in Ricardo's leg.

Ricardo dumped a pair into the shooter's already shot-up face as he hit the floor.

Hannah and Anton by the odd grouping of shots—Hannah's almost stacked with his, spine cutters at nose high, and Anton's single high on the skull, possibly even skipping off the bone underneath.

Nine rounds left in his lone magazine.

Ricardo slapped a hand on his leg.

It wasn't just bleeding.

It was spurting.

Arterial flow!

He jammed a finger into the bullet hole, which hurt like a firebrand—something he had too much experience with.

But it didn't stop the flow.

Out of the firefight and momentarily protected by still being under the Humvee, he yanked off his belt, wrapped it twice around his upper thigh, and rebuckled it—earning him skinned knuckles as he battered them against the underside of the Humvee's suspension. Jamming the Glock's muzzle through one of the loops, he cranked it around three times. Ricardo couldn't tell if the blood flow stopped, but by the amount of pain, he'd assume it was tight enough. Any tighter and he might pass out from the pain and lose his hold on the weapon.

Another spate of automatic gunfire, this time from the front of the vehicle. If Hannah and Anton were still in the game rather than bleeding out as he was, they'd be pinned down by a shooter who could control either side of the vehicle. Humvee windshields were tough, but they didn't last forever.

He twisted his leg around and fought against the scream of pain that threatened to erupt forth and reveal his position. But he managed to line up his handgun, still wrapped into his belt-tourniquet, by aiming with the angle of his leg. The first shot passed between the shooter's legs. But the second shot hit him. He dropped to one knee, but not to the floor.

It was enough. Ricardo shot him twice in the balls, blowing his hip to smithereens.

This time he had no choice, and just as he had back in the jungle, he screamed; the scream ripped from his lungs despite his best efforts. The repeated jerks of the firing recoil that transmitted into his wound by the tourniquet belt wrapped around his thigh was too much. Then the searing powder burn of the muzzle flash scorching across the open wound and blowing down the leg of his pants struck home.

When someone dragged him out from underneath the Humvee, he was past caring if it was Hannah and Anton or the security squad turned drug runners.

"Gonna haveta rescue your sorry ass again, Ricardo. Gettin' to be a goddamn habit."

Anton.

Then he looked down at Ricardo's leg and for a second Ricardo was afraid that Anton was going to faint and land on top of him.

MICHELLE CAME to with a monotone scream sounding in her head as she was jostled hard against some soft surface.

She reached up to cover her ears, but couldn't.

Her hands were zip-tied together.

The scream might have been her own. Or imagined.

Another slam threw her into—Jesse's back. They were lying side by side in a fast-moving vehicle. On a very, very rough road.

That's when the throbbing kicked in. Raising both hands together, she was able to find the swelling lump on her skull. Then the incredible pain of her jaw.

The image came back of a fist connecting with her chin and her collapsing like a rag doll. Some hero she was.

Triage.

She had no arterial blood flow, no bleeding at all that she could find.

And she was breathing normally despite a cloth tied over her mouth. She couldn't seem to find the knot, which must be behind her head. So the scream hadn't been hers.

Shock? Maybe.

No nausea (good thing since she was gagged). Breathing normal. Her own skin didn't feel cool or moist. More hot, like she was being slowly roasted alive.

She tried counting backward from ten, just to see if she could.

At seven, the scream sounded again. Definitely not her. Only one person could scream inside her head other than her.

:Goddamn you to hell, Ricardo.:

Nothing.

Michelle tried to glare at Ricardo, except—oh right, he wasn't here.

Instead she was staring at Jesse from mere inches away. His eyes were closed, but the gag over his mouth only proved that the scream hadn't been his either. He was bound hand and foot and the two of them were in some cramped space that she finally decided was the rear equipment area of the Humvee. She wasn't being roasted, just lying in the back of a sunbaked Humvee.

She nudged him, but he didn't wake up. Crashing through a pothole that must be as big as the Humvee slammed them together—still he was unresponsive. They were close enough that she could hear his steady breathing. Still alive.

He looked pretty battered: a lot of little cuts, and his left eye was bruising badly. The lividity told her she'd been out only briefly. Probably less than ten minutes. He'd fought hard and paid the price.

:Go suck an egg, Ricardo. My head hurts, leave me alone.:

:Why?:

:Because I asked you to. Or is that too difficult a concept for you?:

:No, I mean why does your head hurt?: His words seemed to stutter into her head with strange gaps.

:From having my head smashed against the runway. Now leave me alone.:

:Can't. Need help.:

:The great Ricardo Manella, Mr. I-Don't-Need-Anybody, wants my help? (shocked query) Well tough, I'm all tied up at the moment.:

:I'm bleeding. How do I stop it?:

:Try a Band-Aid. I've been knocked out and now I'm tied up in back of a Humvee with Jesse. Help yourself a little, baby.:

:Shit! Shit! Shit!:

Michelle came awake enough to try her feet…but they were bound together as well. *:You could come rescue me, you know.:*

:At the rate. I'm bleeding out. Not alive long enough.:

:WHAT?: At least it was a shout in her head. *:Were you shot?: Duh, Michelle! :Where? Can you get a tourniquet on it?:*

:Done. Have a med kit. Tell Hannah. Patch me up.:

:How?:

:Through me.:

It was surreal. This time she wasn't guiding her semi-brother in a jungle raid to save Ricardo, who she hadn't met yet. Instead, she was lying beneath the cargo hatch with the only light filtering in from the passenger compartment over the back seat of a racing Humvee. Meanwhile, she was giving step-by-step instructions to Ricardo, to explain to Hannah how to cut his leg open and fix his artery. It wasn't like they could pack it in ice or rush him to a hospital.

When she'd suggested the latter, he'd explained that they were still pinned down. There were gaps in the surgery while Hannah had to join the firefight with Anton.

Michelle felt the shame that she hadn't asked about her semi-brother until that moment. Hannah had asked after Jesse in the first ten seconds and was still asking every minute or so if he was awake yet.

Somehow they did it. The punctured artery was just above the knee, which was a good thing. Close up to the pelvis would be much harder to fix. And punctured was much easier to patch than severed.

Her first-ever patient, and she treated him while lying helplessly on her side in the back of a Humvee racing along in the sun.

:Ease the tourniquet off slowly to check for leaks.:

She held her breath until Ricardo reported all good. Leading them through the closure steps was mostly about antibiotic salve and a tightly wrapped bandage.

:Now stay off it until a real surgeon can check it over and close it properly.:

:Where are you?:

:You're not—: She had no idea why she was arguing. Ricardo, Hannah, and Anton racing to her rescue sounded like a great idea. *:Lounging in the back of a racing Humvee.:*

Any doubts she might have had about the toughness of Delta Force soldiers, which she hadn't had to begin with, were blown away. No sedatives, he'd repeated every medical instruction to make sure he was passing it on correctly. Now, fresh from surgery and probably weak from blood loss, he was preparing to come after her.

:Specifics. Where. Are. You.:

:I'm being bounced around in the back of a Humvee. Jesse's still out cold; they must have taken him down harder than me.:

:Isobel?:

:We offloaded her before anything went down. Docs will know she's a fake now. She'll raise the alarm.:

CHAPTER 17

*W*ell, at least they were talking again. Ricardo would take that as a positive sign.

He puzzled at Michelle's last comment for a moment. Isobel should have alerted someone. Unless…

She was probably in an interrogation room being quizzed about her arrival under false pretenses. And if her delivery pilot and medic had suddenly gone missing, the military would be very suspicious of her. So much for testing the base's security—it would be on full alert now, performing a manhunt for the missing pilot and medic. Except it didn't sound as if they were on base anymore, so that wouldn't be much help.

Isobel would bring them around in time because nothing could stop Izzy's charm when she chose to wield it.

In time.

He didn't have time.

Ricardo lay his head back on the cool concrete for a moment longer, listening to the sporadic back-and-forth gunfire going on around him. They'd made their stand behind a shield of Humvee, airplane, and helicopter tires. The floor was covered in blood. His blood.

Sleep.

He really just wanted to sleep.

But he didn't dare. Forcing himself upright wasn't the most painful thing he'd done this year, but it was very close.

"Sitrep."

"Man wants a situation report, he must be alive," Anton said deadpan without turning from his position scanning through a narrow gap in their tire wall.

"I might have noticed. Hannah?"

"We've got at least one more shooter. Back of the hangar about two o'clock. Can't find him, but he's there."

Ricardo scanned the floor and spotted the guard who he'd shot in the balls to bring him down. He lay nearby and, more importantly, on their side of the rubber tire barricade.

"Anton, grab him."

Anton snaked out a hand and dragged the corpse over.

No need to ask if Hannah was ready; she was Delta.

"Raise him up." Ricardo tipped a rifle—there were several scattered about—on top of the tires, as if he was about to pop his head up for a quick look-see. Then he nodded for Anton to raise the corpse's head above the top of their tire fortress.

Less than a second later, the back of the corpse's head disappeared in a cloud of red blood splatter.

Having revealed his position with his muzzle flash—lying on the roof of a partly disassembled Huey UH-1N helo at the far side of the hangar—Hannah pumped three rounds into him.

The silence seemed to echo off the metal walls.

"We clear?"

"I think so."

Anton tried raising the corpse again, but there were no reactions.

Why hadn't security come to all of the gunfire? Because it had all happened inside a closed aircraft hangar well away from the main section of the base. And because these guys were the base's primary security.

The only sound now was Hannah dumping partly spent magazines and loading full ones. She handed him a pair of Glocks that he slid into his shoulder harness, and a fistful of fresh magazines for his pockets. No time to worry about a vest. The M4 rifle he'd taken off the guard was lifted out of his shaking hands. By the time he got them back under control, Hannah handed the M4 back to him with a pair of thirty-round magazines taped in an alternating up-down pattern for fast changeout.

"Wish I'd had this earlier."

"Yeah, good thing for us we didn't need your help none," Anton teased him.

Hannah said nothing, keeping her attention on the hangar.

With Hannah's help, he managed to regain his feet, but he wouldn't be using the left leg any time soon.

He looked at the Humvee they'd arrived in. It was riddled with bullets, which probably didn't matter—Humvees were designed tough. But the windows had been badly star-cracked. It would be nearly impossible to drive and would raise a lot of unwanted questions from anyone who spotted them.

"We need wheels."

"We'll have other problems in a minute," Hannah nodded toward the main hangar door.

She was right.

"Friendlies?" Anton asked.

"Willing to put money on that?" Hannah kept assembling weapons.

Anton grunted uncertainly.

Ricardo shook his head to clear it. Sweat rolled down his forehead and into his eyes, making them sting. He wished it was heat sweat, but he knew from experience that it was pain sweat.

"If the first to arrive is the security force's contingent from the restaurant, the answer is no. If it's base personnel, the answer is that we just shot the shit out of their security forces, so the answer is still no. Michelle's in trouble, we've got to get moving."

"She *what?*" Anton spun on him. "Mighta mentioned that sooner, asshole."

"I was busy bleeding."

"No fucking excuse."

It wasn't. Even though he'd had no choice, it wasn't. He surveyed the hangar, something he hadn't had a chance to do sooner.

Their, actually Jack Harper's, shattered Humvee had been pulled into a side service bay. In the far corner sat the partly serviced Huey with the dead guy lying on top of it. At least ten bodies were sprawled across the concrete, four of them around the useless Humvee.

And in the exact center sat an UH-60 Black Hawk.

"Anybody hit that?"

"Not me," Hannah shook her head.

Anton just smiled.

BECAUSE THE BASE commander was a fan, Isobel managed to convince him that she was merely part of a test and not a security threat. When she asked about Michelle's and Jesse's whereabouts, she'd lost most of the goodwill she'd felt building between them.

Asking about the second team was a big mistake.

Colonel Jewison scrambled the security detail. The handcuffs, which the first guard had slapped on her, then the colonel had removed, were back on. A corporal now stood with one hand clamped firmly around her biceps as they walked out to inspect the Bell LongRanger her team had rented to deliver her here as a bloody patient.

She tried to reach out, to feel where her people were, but her powers had never extended more that a few dozen meters with the exception of Ricardo. Him she could follow to about half a kilometer. But he was out at her limits; she could feel him, but not what he was feeling.

All she sensed were the nearest soldiers. Some were calm, but many were definitely ready to have something to shoot first and question later. There was an excitement beneath their professional demeanor that she wished she didn't know about.

Should she warn the colonel to rein in his men?

Would he listen if she tried?

Her bet was against it, but she had to try.

"Colonel, I—"

There was a shout down the field.

She turned in time to see a hangar's doors slide open. The instant they were, a Black Hawk helicopter emerged, already in flight a foot off the ground. Whoever had opened the doors ran alongside for a moment and then dove into the open cargo bay door.

Before the tail was fully out of the hangar, the helo was already climbing and turning away to the east.

A pickup truck that had been approaching from the gate squealed to a halt. Four men poured out, then, aiming rifles at the departing helicopter, began firing in long bursts.

"What the hell is Jack Harper up to?" The colonel's snarl had the man next to him reaching for a radio.

She didn't know who Jack Harper was, but he was

obviously one of the four men shooting at the departing helicopter—and they all looked pissed as hell.

Her tenuous contact with Ricardo faded rapidly. He must be aboard that helo. Was that a good thing or bad thing? She had no way to tell.

If that was either Anton or Jesse stealing a helicopter, something had gone far more wrong than she'd feared.

And she knew she was helpless to do anything about it.

CHAPTER 18

:*Can you give me any guidance?*:

Michelle grunted as the Humvee bounced through another pothole. It was not the right prescription for making her head hurt less.

:*Sure. Go find a high cliff. Jump off.*:

:*Later. I promise. Give me something, Michelle.*:

Damn it. He was using her first name again. It meant he really was worried about her. Well, in the moments when she wasn't being scared to death about being kidnapped, she was actually rather pleased. If she was his saving angel, then he could be her avenging demon—because she really needed some hell unleashed on whoever was driving this—

Another pothole plunge followed by washboard road.

:*Dirt road. Bad shape. Moving fast.*:

:*In Honduras? I'm so surprised.*:

She leveraged herself up on Jesse's unresponsive body and peeked over the back of the rear seat—looking straight into the eyes of the driver reflected in the rearview mirror. It was the man who'd struck her to the ground. Beside him, all she could see of the passenger was the rifle he held across his chest with the barrel pointing at the roof.

Michelle ducked back down. *:Two very bad men driving. They look nasty and are heavily armed.:*

:The road. The terrain. What direction is the sun?:

Reaching for the bravery she'd always imagined herself having during EMT drills, she used it to lever herself back up into view. The driver's glare snapped to the mirror once more. This time, the passenger turned to look back at her as well—through his rifle scope. The tip of the barrel was so close she could almost touch it.

She dropped back down on Jesse.

:Do NOT (seriously loud demand) ask me to do that again.:

:What did you see?:

:Sun,: Michelle tried to picture the shooter's face and couldn't. The faceless terror. The gunman had been in shadow. *:Over passenger's right shoulder, behind. Lighting the dashboard, but not him.:*

:Heading northeast. Good, girl.:

:Woman.:

:No argument. What else?:

:Uh, trees. Thick trees. Never been to a jungle, but it looks like one.:

:Can you see anything else?:

Michelle considered what the passenger with the rifle might do if she popped her head up again. *:Is this what it feels like?:*

:What?:

:Terror.: She was sweating far more than she could account for from the heat. Was this day going to end with rape or death? Or both? To never see her semi-brother or laugh with Isobel again. To not find out just what there was between her and Ricardo.

:Breathe. Focus on the moment and breathe. It's the only thing

that gets you through. Here and now. Don't think about the future. Don't think about consequences.:

:A lot you know.: The instant she said it, she wished she could cut out her mental tongue. Ricardo always seemed to bring out the worst in her.

If she wasn't supposed to be dwelling on the future, ten times over Ricardo Manella should not be dwelling on the past. But she seemed to keep throwing it in his face.

:Ricardo, I—:

:Only the present matters.:

:But—:

:Later. Or not at all. Focus on the now. Is there anything else you can tell me?:

:Without being shot? No.:

:I'm such an idiot.:

:No argument from me.: And there went her sharp tongue again.

:Do you have your cell phone?:

She patted her pockets, then for good measure, checked Jesse's with no luck. *:No. And if the driver has them, I wouldn't suggest calling them.:*

:I have an idea, don't go anywhere.:

:As if.: But Michelle could feel he was gone and had never felt so alone in her life.

CHAPTER 19

"*A*nton. Tell me you have a find-phone app that you're sharing with Michelle."

"Yeah. She's always losing the damn thing. Right-hand shirt pocket." Both of his hands were busy flying them northeast from Soto Cano Air Base.

Hannah had taken the copilot's seat so that Ricardo could stretch out his wounded leg in the back. She pulled out Anton's phone and tapped a few keys. Then she pulled out her own and did the same.

"Both her and Jesse's phones are located at Soto Cano. The kidnappers dumped them."

He pulled out his own phone and dialed Isobel. A male voice answered on the third ring, "Who is this?"

"I'm calling for Isobel Manella."

"She is currently under arrest. Who is this?" The man's voice was brusque. Military.

"Let me speak to your commanding officer."

"This *is* the commanding officer. You have three seconds to—"

"Sir. We are members of a task force that was sent in to

test your airbase's security. I am Master Sergeant Ricardo Manella."

"The one who—"

"Yes!" Ricardo chopped him off. It sucked being right. He was always going to be the one remembered for being tortured for a week in the Honduran jungle. Fucking perfect.

"You were investigating *my base* without alerting me?" He sounded pissed. A pissed colonel was never a good thing.

"Please take that up later with Colonel Michael Gibson, the Delta Force commander. Your problem is far more immediate. We entered the base as two three-man squads. My sister, Isobel, was the point person of one team, I was leading the other. We have run afoul of a drug-smuggling ring run by your contracted security team led by a former Green Beret Sergeant Jack Harper."

"Jack Harper? He's my most trusted—"

"You'll find ten dead bodies in Hangar 14, which I'm guessing is assigned solely to Security Teams International's use, along with a very shot-up Humvee filled with unauthorized weapons and several million dollars in cash. I didn't have time to confirm if drugs were present. Now I need you to arrest the man and find out where his smuggling base is loca—"

A burst of gunfire sounded over the phone and cut him off.

:*RICARDO?*: The Humvee was slowing and she was guessing that was a bad sign.

Silence.

:*Ricardo. (Loud shout)!*:

:*Busy.*:

:*They're stopping!*:

:There's a gun battle at Soto Cano.:

:Are you okay?:

:In a helicopter coming for you. But Isobel's in the thick of it.:

Michelle cringed. Isobel in danger was far worse than being in danger herself. It was the worst of all possible worlds. And Ricardo was coming for her?

She couldn't even imagine what that meant.

The Humvee lurched into a final pothole and stopped.

The front doors banged open and then shut.

Should she fight? Could she fight?

Jesse was still out cold.

Would he fight or cower?

Fight.

She prepared herself as well as she could for the moment they opened the rear cargo hatch.

The latch clunked.

Michelle twisted around so that she could kick with her bound feet. She still wore her cowgirl boots and swore she was going to punch the heels hard into someone's face before she went down. She was—

:Don't resist.:

:What? Are you fucking nuts?: The curse was forced out of her as the hatch swung up and she'd missed her moment. They grabbed her by the rope around her boots and dragged her out over Jesse like the limp fish she was.

How impossibly lame was that.

:Goddamn you, Manella.:

:I think that ship already sailed. Need you to stay conscious. Tell me precisely what you see.:

She managed only one glance around before they dragged her into a steel storage shed. It didn't look good.

CHAPTER 20

*R*icardo's attention whipsawed back and forth.

Gunfire over the phone.

Michelle describing what she'd seen.

Passing on the message to Hannah that Jesse was still alive and still unconscious. Even *her* Delta-born reserve was cracking badly.

Unable to pay attention to everything, he finally chose Michelle.

:Now tell me again what you saw. Details.:

He passed it on word for word to Anton in hopes that he could do one of his remote viewing things and pin down Michelle's location. He didn't hold out much hope. She'd been under a canopy of dense trees and mostly what she'd noticed were the two men dragging her and Jesse out of the Humvee.

"Hang on," Anton began punching some buttons on the helo's console. "Gotta set up on autopilot, since neither of you mere Deltas can fly. Hannah, you keep a lookout and tell me if I'm about to fly into something. I can't 'look' and see at the same time."

That was interesting.

He described Michelle's brief glimpse again. Asked her for more details when Anton asked, but she hadn't anything more.

There might not be intonation in their telepathy, but still he could hear that the panic was rising and would soon overwhelm her.

"Nothing, bro," Anton sounded devastated as he rested his hands back on the controls. "It just isn't enough."

"Ricardo?" Isobel's voice over the phone snapped his attention back to Soto Cano Air Base.

"You're okay?"

"Handcuffed, but fine. All I got was a graze on the arm. Barely bleeding."

Ricardo wanted to throw up. Somehow, he didn't know how, but somehow he should have been there to save her.

"You won't be getting anything from Harper. He shot the colonel, and the Army's own forces are hunting him right now. The other three on his squad are already dead."

"Shit!"

"Go rescue Michelle."

"I don't know how to find her," he could hear his own desperation.

"Remember why we were sent. We—"

She was cut off by another round of gunfire.

"Still safe. Now go save the woman you love."

"The woman I *what?*"

"Time to stop fooling around, Ricardo." And Isobel hung up.

The woman I... Later, Manella. Later. Focus on the now.

Isobel was surrounded by the combined troops of Joint Task Force-Bravo. Michelle was surrounded by desperate drug smugglers on the run.

:*Isobel is safe,*: he prayed to God he was right.

~

*THE WOMAN HE...*WHAT? Michelle had caught that snippet of Ricardo's thoughts. Then he spoke to himself, pushing aside the thought and focusing on the now just as he'd instructed her.

She'd...:*Hey. I heard you.*:

:*What do you mean?*:

:*I mean I heard your thoughts just then. You thought 'The woman I...' I heard that.*:

:*How? I didn't send it. I'm sure I didn't.*:

Michelle considered trying to explain and then thought better of it. That he didn't understand also meant that he didn't get pieces of her own internal dialog. Which was definitely a good thing.

:*Look, Ricardo. What it means is that you're nearby.*:

:*How close?*:

:*I don't know. Usually it only works when I can see you.*:

:*Can you see our helicopter?*:

:*I'm locked in a dark, windowless shed that's probably crawling with spiders.*:

There was a long pause. :*Can you hear our helicopter?*:

She listened. There was a lot of other noise. Generators, what might be barrels banging together, something that definitely sounded like magazines being loaded into weapons.

And in the background...fading away...

:*You passed me. Your sound is fading.*:

Moments later, the helicopter noise grew louder. She could feel hope surge. Maybe—

The shed roared!

Nearby gunfire rattled the thin metal walls. Echoes overwhelmed the small space.

The scream ripped from her throat.

There was no stopping it. Even the gag didn't seem to muffle it.

They were going to kill Ricardo. The world… Screw the world! Her life would be such a worse place if he died.

The gunfire tapered off.

:Well, at least we know where you are now.:

:Fine.: She gasped desperately through her nose. *:So come get me already.:*

:Hang in there, Michelle. I'm working on it.:

Again, what choice did she have?

CHAPTER 21

*R*icardo didn't dare have Anton shoot down at the drug smuggler's camp. Not until they knew exactly where Michelle and Jesse were confined.

And there was no way to do that from a hundred meters above the jungle canopy.

Out of ideas, he looked around the helicopter's cargo bay hoping for some miracle. A TV screen that would show a detailed layout of the camp would be nice.

But this was a medical bird. It had some weapons, but the pair of mounted miniguns was going to do him no more good than the rocket pod or chain gun mounted on the helo's exterior. A pair of folded-up litters were tied to the ceiling. Two large med bags hung at the aft end of the cargo bay. Nothing in there for attacking a heavily armed camp. For that he needed…

Goddamn it! He needed to be able to drop down into the jungle and do what Delta Force did. Go in with a small strike force and take them down—hard!

Except he couldn't walk on his leg without risking tearing everything open again. To do that he'd need a lot more than the bandage Hannah had wrapped around his thigh. He'd need—

Ricardo dove for the med bags and yanked down the zippers. The blood loss shakes were still a problem but he managed.

There it all was.

He ignored all the painkillers. He could really use some but pain he knew how to deal with and he didn't dare dull his thinking or reflexes.

All the bags of intravenous fluids were probably what he needed most. Except he was lacking knowledge and time. Definitely no time for some intravenous drip.

:Hey, Michelle. Can I drink any of the fluids in a med kit to boost my system?:

:You'd probably barf up the saline solution. You can drink the bags labeled 'Lactated Ringers,' but it will taste awful.:

He spotted the bag, sliced open the top with the knife strapped to his good thigh, and chugged it back. Better than chewing painkillers. Thinking of which, he spotted a bottle of acetaminophen and chewed a couple of them to get the fastest punch. Yep! Definitely worse than Ringers.

The last was a SAM Splint. He shaped the thick, flexible material around his lower thigh and strapped it down hard. At least if he started bleeding again, it wouldn't be spraying all over the place. And it just might let him use the leg.

"Anton. Find us a clearing within a kilometer of their camp. Hannah and I are going for a walk."

"You're what? Bro, you are so full of shit. I've seen the *inside* of your leg and it wasn't a pretty sight."

Hannah's response was to crawl out of the copilot's seat and into the back of the helo. She began organizing weapons.

"Michelle and Jesse are alive, but their life expectancy is very short. We're going in. Now get us down."

"Well, we're screwed, bro. Nothing open for a couple miles around."

Ricardo pointed at a Fast Rope. The forty-millimeter rope hung in a thick coil.

Hannah slid back the cargo bay door and hooked the rope to an outer attachment point.

Anton groaned over the headset. "Okay, okay. I'll find you a spot for that."

Hannah had begun handing over rifles, grenades, and other useful toys by the time Anton called back.

"Kick the rope."

Hannah kicked the coil and it spilled out the door.

Anton was hovering with the Black Hawk's wheels in the trees, but the cargo door was over a narrow gap.

Hannah pulled on heavy gloves and went first.

Ricardo wasn't so sure of his control, so he let her get halfway down before he followed.

Hannah caught his waist just before his feet hit the ground, easing the impact on his leg.

In the damn jungle again.

"Down," Ricardo announced over the radio headset he'd slid on. Even as he and Hannah moved away, there was a snakelike hiss from Anton hit the rope release and it coiling down to the jungle floor.

:We're coming for you, Michelle.:
:You get killed and I'll be some kind of seriously pissed.:
:Nothing new there.:

HE WAS RIGHT. She'd been focusing a lot of anger in his direction.

How much of it did he deserve? And how much of it was

her notorious Missy-tantrums that Anton was always teasing her about?

She wished she could recall what Isobel had said on the flight down, but all of that seemed to belong to a different life. A life before she was punched out and kidnapped. A life before she understood what being truly afraid felt like.

Fear wasn't not making the dress sale, but she'd always known that.

She'd expected to feel fear of losing a patient when she'd been doing training shifts in various hospital ERs. But none of them touched what she'd experienced in the six days leading up to Ricardo's rescue.

Now the tables were turned and here she was. At least she was unharmed. Kidnapped perhaps an hour ago compared to Ricardo's days of suffering.

Yet the terror slid across her like a freezing shadow that chilled her to the very core.

This, *this!* is what Ricardo had been through. For hopeless days on end. Plus torture.

But she also recalled how amazing he'd been, moving through the Range 37 shoot house with Hannah.

She took strength from that. He'd found his way through something much worse than this. Not only that, but he'd become the man he was despite all of it.

Actually—she thought back to Isobel's stories when they'd roomed together in college—he'd always been that way. He might worship his big twin sister, but there was no question that their love went both ways.

To be a part of that.

To somehow share in even a thin slice of it couldn't help but be a very good thing. She'd probably never find a better man even if she—

A burst of gunfire had her yelping into her gag again.

Shouts and return gunfire sounded outside the shed walls.

:Stay low (command).:

He wouldn't get any argument from her this time. She did her best to meld with the shed's dirt floor.

CHAPTER 22

*T*he sweat streaming down his face and the lancing pain of every step fell away as the situation went dynamic.

He and Hannah had planned as well as they could. They'd called up to Anton with both of their GPS locations—at least their starting locations—and the location of the shed close beside the parked Humvee. He'd map those and avoid hitting them from above.

Thankfully, there was only the one Humvee, as there were many sheds and buildings under the sweltering trees, some little better than hovels.

Ricardo wanted someone high in the trees to get the best possible angle, but the memory of being shot in the trees with nowhere to go but down made him reject that option.

That and Kee's reminder to keep the team tight.

Except that just wasn't going to be possible taking on a whole camp with only two of them.

He sent Hannah off wide to the right. Hopefully the drug camp would think that a force far larger than two people were coming at them because the gunfire would be coming in from two points ninety degrees apart.

Sure enough, the smugglers began shooting up the middle.

Each shot they fired revealed another shooter's location for him and Hannah. M4s weren't the best sniper rifles, but they'd moved within fifty meters of the camp, making them plenty effective. Flash suppressors effectively masked and silenced their own shots. In quick succession, every unfriendly in the camp who fired dropped to the ground dead moments later.

Hannah had suggested they divide the field of fire to avoid wasting time with multiple shots on the same target, and it was working.

A stream of workers raced off into the jungle.

Not their concern.

The security forces were not slouches. Probably all ex-military, they soon formed up and created protective perimeters.

That's when he called in an airstrike from Anton. All alone in a helo that really called for two pilots, especially when firing weapons, he kept the engagements limited.

"Hydra 70 at seventy degrees magnetic and thirty meters from my beacon."

Moments later an angry rocket's hiss sounded close above the canopy of trees. The 2.75-inch-wide and four-foot-long rocket went supersonic right out of the launcher. Before the sound even had time to fully develop, it plowed into the edge of the enemy's gathering point. Bodies, at least parts of bodies, were flung up into the air.

MICHELLE COWERED as some explosion punched holes through the upper part of the shed. Sunlight streamed into the darkness.

In the light, she could see Jesse was awake and struggling to sit up.

She couldn't speak through the gag to tell him to stay down. She threw herself at him and knocked him back to the dirt hard enough that he groaned loudly.

She'd apologize later.

The door flung open.

It didn't need any blinking against the sudden brightness to recognize who stood in the doorway.

As loud as she could in her head, she screamed.

:Ricardo!:

RICARDO HAD NEVER BEFORE HAD the volume of the telepathy change. This time it was so loud that his ears were ringing in sympathy, even though Michelle's cry hadn't passed through them.

The shed door was behind the Humvee.

He could see that it was now open, but he couldn't get an angle on it.

"Cover me!"

He could only pray that Hannah heard his shout.

Ricardo ducked low and broke into a sprint.

He dumped the M4 rifle—empty and no time to slot a fresh magazine—and pulled out his two Glock pistols as he ran.

Even if Hannah hadn't heard him, she'd seen he was on the move and he could hear her bullets passing close by as she laid down protective fire.

His wounded leg was lost somewhere back in the land of adrenaline. He'd gladly pay the price in pain later.

As he neared the Humvee, a round plowed into the ground close in front of him. But it didn't come from the direction of the camp. Hannah had shot exactly where his next step would be.

Danger ahead!

All the warning he needed.

He dove for the ground and rolled, once again ending up beneath a Humvee. This just wasn't going to be his day.

That's when he spotted the sky-blue cowgirl boots, tied together and dragging along the ground.

Dragging between a pair of legs dressed in camos and Army boots.

Ricardo shot one of the Army boots.

With a cry, the man dropped Michelle—then collapsed behind her.

No good angle.

No way to know who else was still in the game.

And no time to think about it. Ricardo knew the priorities in his life without thought.

He rolled out from under the Humvee. Let the roll turn into kneeling position—his leg managed to fire a massive jolt of pain through the adrenalin, but he ignored it.

With a clear line of fire over Michelle's prone form, he executed the drug smuggler who'd kidnapped her. Not with one round, or even the more traditional three shots a Delta operator used.

He dumped the remaining fourteen rounds into the guy.

When he stopped, there were no other sounds.

Hannah had stopped firing; no one was firing back.

Michelle lay unmoving in fetal position by his feet.

She flinched and opened her eyes when he sliced her hands free.

He didn't need any words as she threw herself against him.

Which was too much for his leg and he went over backward hard, banging his head against the Humvee.

CHAPTER 23

"The ribs at the BBQ Pit are the best," Michelle bit into one to fill her mouth because she was afraid of what might come spilling out.

Screams?

Gibberish?

Begging for…she had no idea what?

Twenty-four hours ago she'd been within seconds of dying in the Honduran jungle, just as Ricardo had almost done.

But Ricardo had saved her.

Since then, she'd had to patch Ricardo's leg together again long enough to deliver him to the medics at Soto Cano. There'd been so many debriefing sessions that she couldn't recall if it had taken three hours or thirteen. It had felt like thirty.

Ricardo, once they'd pumped two units of blood into him and a proper surgeon had seen to his leg, was doing better than the colonel who'd caught three rounds to the gut from Jack Harper. Understandably, Ricardo had refused to stay in Honduras one minute longer than necessary. Since Jack

Harper was still at large, that definitely sounded like a good idea to her.

They hadn't spoken a single word since, aloud or not. Of course, Ricardo had gone from surgery to knocked-out by major painkillers on a litter carried aboard the C-130 Hercules Gibson had sent down to fetch them.

Once back home in San Antonio, he'd refused to be carried off the plane. It had taken Isobel to force him into a wheelchair.

Michelle had wanted to be the one to hold his hand on the flight home, but Isobel had looked so freaked when she'd seen them rushing Ricardo off the helicopter and into surgery that Michelle had just stayed out of the way.

Apparently the only way Isobel had managed to get Ricardo to accept the wheelchair was by promising him ribs at the BBQ Pit. The Pit looked just like it always did: sad. Splitting leatherette bench seats around battered Formica tables. The three items on the menu kept the choices simple: beef ribs, brisket, and pork ribs. She didn't know why they bothered with the last in Texas, maybe for foreigners from Oklahoma or Louisiana. The Coca-Cola tap on the coke machine had recently been taped over, which left only the Dr. Pepper one. Again, all they really needed.

They were also the best ribs she'd ever had.

The chef had taken one look at Jesse's battered face and Ricardo in a wheelchair before announcing, "On the house." He and Anton had traded fist bumps. Old Army buddies, she remembered.

Anton waved a rib at Ricardo. "The colonel renamed you."

"Something other than 'that guy who got tortured'?"

"Yeah. Some shit about calling you a one-man Army. Like Hannah and I were just shucking corn."

"Well, we know that's all *you* were doing," Hannah agreed. "What did you fire, one piddly little rocket?"

"Yeah, but it was righteous shot."

Michelle remembered the shrapnel punching holes through the top of the metal shed and she wondered just how close Anton had come to killing her. She supposed that he'd missed by enough, which was all that mattered in the end.

"Need to find you a woman who won't mind all your shortcomings," Ricardo added his voice to the conversation for the first time.

"Hey, he's back. Welcome aboard, bro."

"God, I hate drugs. What am I on?"

"Mostly oxycodone." One thing Michelle had absolutely tracked were the meds they'd given him.

"Done with that shit."

"But you need it for the pain, Ricardo."

:Drop it, Michelle.:

:But—:

:I've already spent too much of my last year drugged out of caring about anything.:

She couldn't argue with that. "So now that you can, what are you going to care about?"

All conversation around the table ground to an immediate halt as everyone turned to look at her.

"Whoops. I guess that was my out-loud voice."

"Kinda!" Anton scoffed.

Jesse looked puzzled.

Isobel and Hannah shared a common look...that she couldn't interpret at all.

:Sorry. Didn't mean to put you on the spot.:

"Look, they're doing their thing again."

She ignored Anton.

:There is one thing I really care about more than all the rest put together.:

:What?:

:Thought that was kinda obvious.:

Michelle couldn't look away from the intensity of Ricardo's gaze. Those dark, beautiful eyes that always seemed to be watching her.

:You don't mean...:

No way.

:You couldn't...:

But he didn't look aside.

:But you called me an effing civilian.:

He barked an out a loud laugh, but showed no chagrin for interrupting everyone at the table again. *:That's what you get for listening to my thoughts. I was calling myself (emphasis) a fucking civilian.:*

:Why would you do that?: She took a lesson from him and ignored that everyone was watching them.

:I am a civilian in all the worst ways.:

:Colonel said you were a one-man army.:

Ricardo shrugged uncomfortably. No stray thoughts for her to read.

:Seriously. You saved everyone. Even Hannah was impressed.: "Weren't you?" Michelle turned to Hannah.

"Wasn't I what?"

"Oh, never mind." *:She was.:*

Ricardo did more of his silent soldier thing. But neither was he focusing on his meal, looking at the others, or about to fall asleep—even with the drugs still pumping through his system.

:Me?:

He remained still. Not as if refusing to speak, but more as if he was afraid to. The man who had charged one-legged into the middle of a jungle battle to save her actually looked afraid of... Her? Of what she might answer?

:Ricardo! I'm not some perfect angel of mercy.:

:No, you're better than that, you're a real live flesh and blood one.:

:No, I'm—:

:An EMT who saved my life. Again. But that's not what counts.:

:What does?: Michelle realized that she was perched on the edge of her seat and leaning as close as his wheelchair allowed.

:Michelle. My lovely Michelle. Do you think that over the last year I haven't gotten to know you at least as well as you've gotten to know me?:

That rocked her back in her seat. Could she ever know any man better? Or care about one more? Ricardo's every action—even more, every thought—spoke so clearly of who he was. Brave, loyal, loving.

Who else could she ever care for? *:Say it.:*

His eyes flickered to the table, then he finally broke eye contact, looking down.

:So brave in action...:

Again the uncertain shrug.

:So just tell me.:

Ricardo looked up at her once again. And just a small quirk of a smile caught the corner of his mouth.

Taking the invitation, she leaned in and kissed him.

Just as their lips met, a thought whispered into her head.

:Love you, Michelle Bowman.:

Even if she couldn't hear it on the outside, it was all she needed to hear on the inside.

∼

IF YOU ENJOYED this book and want to really help the author, reviewing this title at the site(s) of your choice would be greatly appreciated.

If you enjoyed this title, you'll love the Night Stalkers 5E series (a sample follows).

Target of the Heart
Target Lock on Love
Target of Mine
Target of One's Own

IF YOU LIKED THIS, YOU'LL LOVE:

The Night Stalkers 5E romances

TARGET OF THE HEART (EXCERPT)

*M*ajor Pete Napier hovered his MH-47G Chinook helicopter ten kilometers outside of Lhasa, Tibet and a mere two inches off the tundra. A mixed action team of Delta Force and The Activity—the slipperiest intel group on the planet—flung themselves aboard.

The additional load sent an infinitesimal shift in the cyclic control in his right hand. The hydraulics to close the rear loading ramp hummed through the entire frame of the massive helicopter. By the time his crew chief could reach forward to slap an "all secure" signal against his shoulder, they were already ten feet up and fifty out. That was enough altitude. He kept the nose down as he clawed for speed in the thin air at eleven thousand feet.

"Totally worth it," one of the D-boys announced as soon as he was on the Chinook's internal intercom.

He'd have to remember to tell that to the two Black Hawks flying guard for him...when they were in a friendly country and could risk a radio transmission. This deep inside China—or rather Chinese-held territory as the CIA's mission-briefing spook had insisted on calling it—radios attracted attention and were only used to avoid imminent death and destruction.

"Great, now I just need to get us out of this alive."

"Do that, Pete. We'd appreciate it."

He wished to hell he had a stealth bird like the one that had gone into bin Laden's compound. But the one that had crashed during that raid had been blown up. Where there was one, there were always two, but the second had gone back into hiding as thoroughly as if it had never existed. He hadn't heard a word about it since.

The Tibetan terrain was amazing, even if all he could see of it was the monochromatic green of night vision. And blackness. The largest city in Tibet lay a mere ten kilometers away and they were flying over barren wilderness. He could crash out here and no one would know for decades unless some yak herder stumbled upon them. Or were yaks in Mongolia? He was a corn-fed, white boy from Colorado, what did he know about Tibet? Most of the countries he'd flown into on Black Ops missions he'd only seen at night anyway.

While moving very, very fast.

Like now.

The inside of his visor was painted with overlapping readouts. A pre-defined terrain map, the best that modern satellite imaging could build made the first layer. This wasn't some crappy, on-line, look-at-a-picture-of-your-house display. Someone had a pile of dung outside their goat pen? He could see it, tell you how high it was, and probably say if they were pygmy goats or full-size LaManchas by the size of their shit-pellets if he zoomed in.

On top of that were projected the forward-looking infrared camera images. The FLIR imaging gave him a real-time overlay, in case someone had put an addition onto their goat shed since the last satellite pass or parked their tractor across his intended flight path.

His nervous system was paying autonomic attention to that combined landscape. He also compensated for the thin air at altitude as he instinctively chose when to start his climb over said goat shed or his swerve around it.

It was the third layer, the tactical display that had most of his attention. At least he and the two Black Hawks flying escort on him were finally on the move.

To insert this deep into Tibet, without passing over Bhutan or Nepal, they'd had to add wingtanks on the Black Hawks' hardpoints where he'd much rather have a couple banks of Hellfire missiles. Still, they had 20 mm chain guns and the crew chiefs had miniguns which was some comfort. His twin-rotor Chinook might be the biggest helicopter that the Night Stalkers flew, but it was the cargo van of Special Operations and only had two miniguns and a machine gun of its own. Though he'd put his three crew chiefs up against the best Black Hawk shooter any day.

While the action team was busy infiltrating the capital city and gathering intelligence on the particularly brutal Chinese assistant administrator, Pete and his crews had been squatting out in the wilderness under a camouflage net designed to make his helo look like just another god-forsaken Himalayan lump of granite.

Command had determined that it was better for the helos to wait on site through the day than risk flying out and back in. He and his crew had stood shifts on guard duty, but none of them had slept. They'd been flying together too long to have any new jokes, so they'd played a lot of cribbage. He'd long ago ruled no gambling on a mission, after a fistfight had broken out about a bluff hand that cost a Marine three hundred and forty-seven dollars. Marines hated losing to Army no matter how many times it happened. They'd had to sit on him for a long time before he calmed down.

Tonight's mission was part of an on-going campaign to discredit the Chinese "presence" in Tibet on the international stage—as if occupying the country the last sixty-plus years didn't count toward ruling, whether invited or not. As usual, there was a crucial vote coming up at the U.N.—that, as usual, the Chinese could be guaranteed to ignore. However, the ever-hopeful CIA was in a hurry to make sure that any damaging information that they could validate was disseminated as thoroughly as possible prior to the vote.

Not his concern.

His concern was, were they going to pass over some Chinese sentry post at their top speed of a hundred and ninety-six miles an hour? The sentries would then call down a couple Shenyang J-16 jet fighters that could hustle along at Mach 2—over fifteen *hundred* mph—to fry his sorry ass. He knew there was a pair of them parked at Lhasa along with some older gear that would be just as effective against his three helos.

"Don't suppose you could get a move on, Pete?"

"Eat shit, Nicolai!" He was a good man to have as a copilot. Pete knew he was holding on too tight, and Nicolai knew that a joke was the right way to ease the moment.

He, Nicolai, and the four pilots in the two Black Hawks had a long way to go tonight and he'd never make it if he stayed so tight on the controls that he could barely maneuver. Pete eased off and felt his fingers tingle with the rush of returning blood. They dove down into gorges and followed them as long as they dared. They hugged cliff walls at every opportunity to decrease their radar profile. And they climbed.

That was the true danger—they would be up near the helos' limits when they crossed over the backbone of the Himalayas in their rush for India. The air was so rarefied that they burned fuel at a prodigious rate. Their reserve didn't allow for any extended battles while crossing the border...not for any battle at all really.

IT WAS pitch dark outside her helicopter when Captain Danielle Delacroix stamped on the left rudder pedal while giving the big Chinook right-directed control on the cyclic. It tipped her most of the way onto her side but let her continue in a straight line. A Chinook's rotors were sixty feet across—front to back they overlapped to make the spread a hundred feet long. By cross-controlling her bird to tip it, she managed to execute a straight line between two mock pylons only thirty feet apart. They were made of thin cloth so they wouldn't down the helo if you sliced one—she was the only trainee to not have cut one yet.

At her current angle of attack, she took up less than a half-rotor of width, just twenty-four feet. That left her nearly three feet to either side, sufficient as she was moving at under a hundred knots.

The training instructor sitting beside her in the copilot's seat didn't react as she swooped through the training course at Fort Campbell, Kentucky. Only child of a single mother, she was used to providing her own feedback loops, so she didn't expect anything else. Those who expected outside validation rarely survived the SOAR induction testing, never mind the two years of training that followed.

As a loner kid, Danielle had learned that self-motivated congratulations and fun were much easier to come by than external ones. She'd spent innumerable hours deep in her mind as a pre-teen superheroine. At twenty-nine she was well on her way to becoming a real life one, though Helo-girl had never been a character she'd thought of in her youth.

External validation or not, after two years of training with the U.S. Army's 160th Special Operations Aviation Regiment she was ready for some action. At least *she* was convinced that she was. But the trainers of Fort Campbell, Kentucky had not signed off on anyone in her trainee class yet. Nor had they given any hint of when they might.

She ducked ten tons of racing Chinook under a bridge and bounced into a near vertical climb to clear the power line on the far side. Like a ride on the toboggan at Terrassee Dufferin during *Le Carnaval de Québec,* only with ten thousand horsepower at her fingertips. Using her Army signing bonus—the first money in her life that was truly hers —to attend *Le Carnaval* had been her one trip back to her birthplace since her mother took them to America when she was ten.

To even apply to SOAR required five years of prior military rotorcraft experience. She had applied after seven years because of a chance encounter—or rather what she'd thought was a chance encounter at the time.

Captain Justin Roberts had been a top Chinook pilot, the one who had convinced her to switch from her beloved Black Hawk and try out the massive twin-rotor craft. One flight and she'd been a goner, begging her commander until he gave in and let her cross over to the new platform. Justin had made the jump from the 10th Mountain Division to the 160th SOAR not long after that.

Then one night she'd been having pizza in Watertown, New York a couple miles off the 10th's base at Fort Drum.

"Danielle?" Justin had greeted her with the surprise of finding a good friend in an unexpected place. Danielle had always liked Justin—even if he was a too-tall, too-handsome cowboy and completely knew it. But "good friend" was unusual for Danielle, with anyone, and Justin came close.

"Captain Roberts," as a dry greeting over the top edge of her Suzanne Brockmann novel didn't faze him in the slightest.

"Mind if I join ya?" A question he then answered for himself by sliding into the opposite seat and taking a slice of her pizza. She been thinking of taking the leftovers back to base, but that was now an idle thought.

"Are you enjoying life in SOAR?" she did her best to appear a normal, social human, a skill she'd learned by rote. *Greeting someone you knew after a time apart? Ask a question about them.* "They treating you well?"

"Whoo-ee, you have no idea, Danielle," his voice was smooth as…well, always…so she wouldn't think about it also sounding like a pickup line. He was beautiful but didn't interest her; the outgoing ones never did.

"Tell me." *Men love to talk about themselves, so let them.*

And he did. But she'd soon forgotten about her novel and would have forgotten the pizza if he hadn't reminded her to eat.

His stories shifted from intriguing to fascinating. There was a world out there that she'd been only peripherally aware of. The Night Stalkers of the 160th SOAR weren't simply better helicopter pilots, they were the most highly-trained and best-equipped ones anywhere. Their missions were pure razor's edge and Black Op dark.

He'd left her with a hundred questions and enough interest to fill out an application to the 160th Special Operations Aviation Regiment (airborne). Being a decent guy, Justin even paid for the pizza after eating half.

The speed at which she was rushed into testing told her

that her meeting with Justin hadn't been by chance and that she owed him more than half a pizza next time they met. She'd asked after him a couple of times since she'd made it past the qualification exams—and the examiners' brutal interviews that had left her questioning her sanity, never mind her ability.

"Justin Roberts is presently deployed, ma'am," was the only response she'd ever gotten.

Now that she was through training—almost, had to be soon, didn't it?—Danielle realized that was probably less of an evasion and more likely to do with the brutal op tempo the Night Stalkers maintained. The SOAR 1st Battalion had just won the coveted Lt. General Ellis D. Parker awards for Outstanding Combat Aviation Battalion *and* Aviation Battalion of the Year. They'd been on deployment every single day of the last year, actually of the last decade-plus since 9/11.

The very first Special Forces boots on the ground in Afghanistan were delivered that October by the Night Stalkers and nothing had slacked off since. Justin might be in the 5th battalion D company, but they were just as heavily assigned as the 1st.

Part of the recruits' training had included tours in Afghanistan. But unlike their prior deployments, these were brief, intense, and then they'd be back in the States pushing to integrate their new skills.

SOAR needed her training to end and so did she.

Danielle was ready for the job, in her own, inestimable opinion. But she wasn't going to get there until the trainers signed off that she'd reached fully mission-qualified proficiency. FMQ was the gold star of the Night Stalkers pipeline.

The Fort Campbell training course was never set up the

same from one flight to the next, but it always had a time limit. The time would be short and they didn't tell you what it was. So she drove the Chinook for all it was worth like Regina Jaquess waterskiing her way to U.S. Ski Team Female Athlete of the Year.

The Night Stalkers were a damned secretive lot, and after two years of training, she understood why. With seven years flying for the 10th, she'd thought she was good.

She'd been repeatedly lauded as one of the top pilots at Fort Drum.

The Night Stalkers had offered an education in what it really meant to fly. In the two years of training, she'd flown more hours than in the seven years prior, despite two deployments to Iraq. And spent more time in the classroom than her life-to-date accumulated flight hours.

But she was ready now. It was *très viscérale,* right down in her bones she could feel it. The Chinook was as much a part of her nervous system as breathing.

Too bad they didn't build men the way they built the big Chinooks—especially the MH-47G which were built specifically to SOAR's requirements. The aircraft were steady, trustworthy, and the most immensely powerful helicopters deployed in the U.S. Army—what more could a girl ask for? But finding a superhero man to go with her superhero helicopter was just a fantasy for a lonely girl who'd once had dreams of more.

She dove down into a canyon and slid to a hover mere inches over the reservoir inside the thirty-second window laid out on the flight plan.

Danielle resisted a sigh. She was ready for something to happen and to happen soon.

$\approx$

M. L. BUCHMAN

(Keep reading at fine retailers everywhere)

Target of the Heart
Target Lock on Love
Target of Mine
Target of One's Own

ABOUT THE AUTHOR

M.L. "Matt" Buchman started the first of over 60 novels, 100 short stories, and a fast-growing pile of audiobooks while flying from South Korea to ride his bicycle across the Australian Outback. Part of a solo around the world trip that ultimately launched his writing career in: thrillers, military romantic suspense, contemporary romance, and SF/F.

Recently named in *The 20 Best Romantic Suspense Novels: Modern Masterpieces* by ALA's Booklist, they have also selected his works three times as "Top-10 Romance Novel of the Year." NPR and B&N listed other works as "Best 5 of the Year."

As a 30-year project manager with a geophysics degree who has: designed and built houses, flown and jumped out of planes, and solo-sailed a 50' ketch. He is awed by what's possible. More at: www.mlbuchman.com.

Other works by M. L. Buchman: *(* - also in audio)*

Other works by M. L. Buchman:

Contemporary Romance (cont)

Where Dreams
Where Dreams are Born
Where Dreams Reside
Where Dreams Are of Christmas
Where Dreams Unfold
Where Dreams Are Written

Science Fiction / Fantasy

Deities Anonymous
Cookbook from Hell: Reheated
Saviors 101

Single Titles
The Nara Reaction
Monk's Maze
the Me and Elsie Chronicles

Non-Fiction

Strategies for Success
Managing Your Inner Artist/Writer
Estate Planning for Authors*
Character Voice
Narrate and Record Your Own
Audiobook*

Short Story Series by M. L. Buchman:

Romantic Suspense

Delta Force
Delta Force

Firehawks
The Firehawks Lookouts
The Firehawks Hotshots
The Firebirds

The Night Stalkers
The Night Stalkers
The Night Stalkers 5E
The Night Stalkers CSAR
The Night Stalkers Wedding Stories

US Coast Guard
US Coast Guard

White House Protection Force
White House Protection Force

Contemporary Romance

Eagle Cove
Eagle Cove

Henderson's Ranch
Henderson's Ranch

Where Dreams
Where Dreams

Thrillers

Dead Chef
Dead Chef

Science Fiction / Fantasy

Deities Anonymous
Deities Anonymous

Other
The Future Night Stalkers
Single Titles

Printed in Great
Britain
by Amazon